THE LAIRD'S GUARDIAN ANGEL
HIGHLAND LAIRDS

ELIZA KNIGHT

ABOUT THE BOOK

Laird Alistair Sinclair has been fighting alongside Robert the Bruce for the last few years in the War of Independence for Scotland. Nursing an injury, he makes the journey home from battle, with the intent to put his own lands to rights while he recovers—only Alistair nearly tramples a beguiling lass on his lands before he arrives. She begs him for help, and dangles before him a secret he can't ignore, just as he can't shake the desire that thrums in his veins at the sight of her.

Escaping near death at the treacherous hands of an English soldier who raided her clan's castle, Lady Calliope Ramsey flees to the nearby Sinclair lands, desperate for help and to relay the information she overheard. With the future of her clan and Scotland at stake, she implores her neighbor for aid, all while trying to ignore his striking gaze that sends her heart fluttering.

Can Alistair trust the captivating woman who claims to be his ally? With the battle coming closer to his doorstep, he has little choice but to believe Calliope. Side by side, they will risk everything to protect what is theirs, only to find the one thing they forgot to fortify was their hearts...

MORE BOOKS BY ELIZA KNIGHT

Highland Lairds

The Laird's Prize
The Laird's Kiss
The Laird's Guardian Angel

Distinguished Scots

A Scot's Pride
A Dash of Scot
A Scot's Perfect Match - coming soon

Scots of Honor

Return of the Scot
The Scot is Hers
Taming the Scot

Prince Charlie's Rebels

The Highlander Who Stole Christmas
Pretty in Plaid

Prince Charlie's Angels

The Rebel Wears Plaid
Truly Madly Plaid
You've Got Plaid

The Sutherland Legacy

The Highlander's Gift
The Highlander's Quest
The Highlander's Stolen Bride
The Highlander's Hellion
The Highlander's Secret Vow
The Highlander's Enchantment

The Stolen Bride Series

The Highlander's Temptation
The Highlander's Reward
The Highlander's Conquest
The Highlander's Lady
The Highlander's Warrior Bride
The Highlander's Triumph
The Highlander's Sin
Wild Highland Mistletoe (a Stolen Bride winter novella)
The Highlander's Charm (a Stolen Bride novella)
A Kilted Christmas Wish – a contemporary Holiday spin-off
The Highlander's Surrender
The Highlander's Dare

The Conquered Bride Series

Conquered by the Highlander
Seduced by the Laird
Taken by the Highlander (a Conquered bride novella)
Claimed by the Warrior
Stolen by the Laird
Protected by the Laird (a Conquered bride novella)
Guarded by the Warrior

The MacDougall Legacy Series

Laird of Shadows
Laird of Twilight
Laird of Darkness

Pirates of Britannia: Devils of the Deep

Savage of the Sea
The Sea Devil
A Pirate's Bounty

THE THISTLES AND ROSES SERIES

Promise of a Knight
Eternally Bound
Breath from the Sea

The Highland Bound Series (Erotic time-travel)

Behind the Plaid

Bared to the Laird
Dark Side of the Laird
Highlander's Touch
Highlander Undone
Highlander Unraveled

Touchstone Series

Highland Steam
Highland Brawn
Highland Tryst
Highland Heat

HISTORICAL FICTION

The Mayfair Bookshop
Starring Adele Astaire
Can't We Be Friends
The Queen's Faithful Companion
Confessions of a Grammar Queen - coming soon!

Tales From the Tudor Court

My Lady Viper
Prisoner of the Queen

Ancient Historical Fiction: Coming Soon!

A Day of Fire: a novel of Pompeii
A Year of Ravens: a novel of Boudica's Rebellion

French Revolution

Ribbons of Scarlet: a novel of the French Revolution

CONTEMPORARY WOMEN'S FICTION

Rush Week-coming soon!
Writing as Michelle Brandon

❦

JANUARY 2025

COPYRIGHT © 2025 ELIZA KNIGHT

THE LAIRD'S GUARDIAN ANGEL © 2025 Eliza Knight. ALL RIGHTS RESERVED. No part or the whole of this book may be reproduced, distributed, transmitted or utilized (other than for reading by the intended reader) in ANY form (now known or hereafter invented) without prior written permission by the author. The unauthorized reproduction or distribution of this copyrighted work is illegal, and punishable by law.

THE LAIRD'S GUARDIAN ANGEL is a work of fiction. The characters and events portrayed in this book are fictional and or are used fictitiously and solely the product of the author's imagination. Any similarity to real persons, living or dead, places, businesses, events or locales is purely coincidental.

Cover Design by Dar Albert

PROLOGUE

Scottish border...
Year of Our Lord, 1287

There was magic in sleeping out of doors. Peeking at the stars before nightfall. Merriment at being at a massive celebratory festival. Especially on the first of May. Music tinkled throughout the day, cascading into the night. The feasts were endless, the fountains of cider ever flowing. But there was also discomfort because sleeping in a tent with her family and servants meant no privacy. Not that a young lady was ever really alone.

At all of six-years-old, Lady Calliope Ramsey stepped from her tent at the Beltane festival which had brought dozens of neighboring clans for a week of celebrating and games. Shivers coursed over her skin at the chill in the morning air. Her bare toes stepped onto the crispy morning grass, the dew frozen from the night before. As her tiny toes crunched against the grass, she contemplated turning back around to grab her slippers, but she was in such need of relief that if she were to do so, she very likely wouldn't make it to the cover of the woods to empty her bladder. Papa wouldn't abide an accident. And really, she was too old for such.

The first rays of the sun took the bite off the coolness of the morning. She'd been waiting hours to go, not wanting to trip over those sleeping on the floor to reach the shared chamber pot. Mama had told her not to have that last cup of cider, but the sweetness of the apples had been entirely too tempting. They never had cider at home.

Calliope tucked her dressing gown closer, the fabric not as thick as her cloak, and peeked around the other tents, glad she'd woken before anyone else appeared to be. Her father, Chieftain of the Ramsey Clan, would kill her if he knew she was walking out like this, barely clothed. No shoes on her bare feet. But yesterday, when the young lassies were dancing around the Maypole, they'd all been barefoot, and their linen white gowns looked very much like night clothes.

And perhaps it was silly of her, maybe even reckless, but Calliope was a bit of a daredevil. Well, at least when no one else was looking, and she preferred to act out her tiny rebellions without getting caught.

A lady had to be quiet about such things. As her mother, Mary, Lady Ramsey, had taught her, a lady was refined in all ways. Subdued. Even when showing her talents, she had to do so quietly. Playing the viola, for example, she could only do soft, soothing music. Nothing that might bring about excitement. Dancing, too, had to be slow, barely lifting her limbs. Just the barest hint of a sway. A lady in the Ramsey household did not skip, and leap and twirl like common Highland ladies.

Except yesterday, when no one was looking, Calliope watched mesmerized as the young ladies danced. Behind the cover of her tent, she mimicked their moves until she felt certain she'd bested them.

According to her mother, the worst offense of all would be if a Ramsey lady were to train to defend herself or climb trees.

One could not have calloused and scraped hands. One could not have bulging muscles. One could not perspire.

Calliope glanced down at her hands, to her right middle finger, where she had a permanent callous in the center. Somehow, she'd kept it hidden from her mother, who had long since given up inspecting her hands for their softness. Lady Ramsey would not dare to dream that her daughter would ever disobey her. Besides, more often than not, Calliope wore gloves when she was climbing trees. No scrapes to be seen.

She rubbed a thumb over the callous, the skin hardened over the last year by the string of her bow. Gregor, her father's groom, had been kind enough to teach her how to notch and aim an arrow, going so far as to set up a target inside the barn for her to use when her mother was otherwise occupied. She'd gotten into the habit of waking up earlier than everyone else just to go to the barn and practice.

Someone stirred in the tent behind her, and she rushed behind a tree to finish her business in peace. When she emerged, her mother stood outside the tent looking frantic. This look she wore so often might have been her permanent expression. The only difference now was the twisting and turning of her head and the running back and forth to look about the tent.

Not wanting to worry her mother much, she hurried until she was spotted, at which point she halted.

"What on earth are you doing, young lady?" Lady Ramsey's English accent grew stronger when she was angry.

She tried to hide it often in Scotland as the English weren't trusted here, not that any of the servants thought her mother to be as evil as the Sassenachs who raided and pillaged. Lady Ramsey might have been strict, but she certainly wasn't evil.

"I didna want to wake ye, mama."

Lady Ramsey sniffed, obviously pleased with her daughter's consideration even if she was peeved.

"A lady does not make use of the bushes unless there is no alternative. Nor does she say *didna* or *ye*. It is *did not* and *you*."

Calliope nodded, not wanting to argue with her mother's flawed logic. Swallowing, she worked her throat and tongue the way she'd been trained and said, "I did not want to wake you, mama."

Lady Ramsey nodded. "Come, we must get ready for the tourney."

Calliope again nodded, following her mother into their tent to prepare for the day. Her hair was brushed to a glossy sheen and swiftly plaited down her back. At least she didn't have to be cinched into a gown like her mother did. Every time the maid tugged, her mother gasped for air as if her clothes made it hard to breathe. Calliope secretly vowed never to be cinched. They had a special place to sit in the makeshift arena. While she didn't always enjoy watching the men hack away at each other, she did love the romanticism of offering her favor to a Scottish warrior.

She slipped a linen square into her sleeve. She'd embroidered a thistle in the corner of it, so if one were to look closely enough, the stem was a bow. Well, perhaps that was giving herself a bit too much credit. After all, she was too young and distracted to have truly made anything that looked like more than a blob. Still, her mother hadn't noticed, and Calliope thought herself rather clever.

In the stands, they took their place beside the other

nobles present. Calliope gazed out over the crowd. Men, women, and children from all around were already cheering for the coming fight. Their gazes were toward the open gate, where a parade of men in their plaids, with targes strapped to their arms to shield themselves from oncoming blows and claymores on their backs, prepared for the first tourney activity, which was swordplay.

She'd been too shy yesterday to offer her favor, but not today. Today, she was going to make a warrior smile.

Later this afternoon, there would be an archery contest, which she would have given anything to be able to participate in. But her mother never took her eyes off of Calliope for long, and if she attempted to sneak away, within a breath she was certain to find the countess or her lady's maid on her heels. Besides, they'd never let a lass into the competition, and since she'd been unable to pack her own trunk, she'd not been able to go through with her plan to pack her cousin Hugh's clothes as a disguise.

A trio of trumpets blew, sending a shockwave of excitement through the crowd. They stood, arms waving in the air. Calliope mimicked their movements, only to feel her mother's sharp pinch on her arm.

"Ladies do not flap."

Calliope sat back down, leaning forward, to peer over the rail at the line of warriors about to show their prowess. The prize was a fortune.

"Sit back, my dear, ladies don't lean."

Calliope bit the inside of her cheek to keep herself from the ready retort, which would only get her banished. She sat back just enough to appease her mother but not all the way as to block her view. She was shorter than the countess, so the rail blocked her somewhat.

Thankfully, Robert the Bruce entered the arena at that

moment, and they all stood in deference, but Calliope used the opportunity to peruse the warriors to see just whom she'd give her favor.

They were all fearsome and strong looking. Arrogant even as they jostled each other, grinning and making what Calliope assumed were lewd jokes, because the countess said that was the only type of joke they knew how to utter. Calliope wasn't sure what lewd meant, but it seemed fun enough.

She tried to keep her face schooled so no one would notice she was eavesdropping, but someone did catch her gaze with eyes the color of a stormy sea. A lad who was holding the reins of a horse near one of the warriors. If she were to follow her mother's rules, Calliope would look away. The ladies did not make eye contact. But her mother had no idea what she was doing, so why not take a peek?

He raised a curious brow at her, and she offered a subtle smile. The lad was tall, she could tell, even from here. His dark hair was cut just above his ears.

He grinned at her, and she couldn't help but smile back. Perhaps it was not a warrior she would bestow her favor on. There was something about the lad that intrigued her. A hint of a daredevil like her. If not for her mother, she might have approached him to see if he wanted to be her friend.

Perhaps that was a bit much, but she felt he would make a good friend and champion, especially as he knew she was listening. That she wanted to be more than the wee lady sitting on the dais, but instead, be the lady riding the horse he was leading. Or perhaps, again, her imagination was running away with her. Calliope definitely did have an overactive imagination. But what lass didn't daydream?

She glanced at her mother. Lady Ramsey probably did not daydream.

As the warriors and the young lad drew closer, her mother

greeted the men. The lad glanced up at Calliope, a smile playing on his lips that she easily returned.

"My lady." He bowed low in front of her, and the countess gasped, clucking her tongue, while the warrior in front of the lad gave a sharp rap.

But before he could be dragged off, and her mother could pinch her again, Calliope slipped the lad her handkerchief. "Until we meet again."

I

Scottish Lowlands
1302

There was no lonelier place for a lady than living in a castle where she was unwanted, in an unfamiliar land.

Unfortunately for Lady Calliope Ramsey, that had been how she'd felt for most of her life.

She was the eldest daughter of Alaric, Chieftain of the Ramsey clan. Currently, she was seated at the end of the long trestle table, staring into the face of a man she didn't remember but was supposed to be her father. And he was scowling. Scowling as if she'd arrived with eight heads and eels for arms.

Despite the manners that had been drilled into her since she was a young girl, Calliope couldn't help giving him quite a similar look. After all, she had always imagined her father, a war hero, to be strapping, the image of Hercules. The man before her now had a face full of white beard and deep grooves within his cheeks. A paunch to his front, though his arms and legs did appear to be the size of tree trunks. That certainly fit the Herculean fantasy of a father.

Nevertheless, what was he scowling at? She wasn't unpleasant to look at. Calliope wasn't vain, but she had seen herself in the looking glass and determined that someday, someone might find her to be attractive enough to wed.

However, that seemed quite unlikely now. There'd not been a single smile for her since she'd crossed the border and been essentially dropped on her father's doorstep by her stepsire in England. Though now that she thought about it, was he really her stepsire if her sire was still alive?

There'd barely been an hour to mourn her mother before her stepsire had ordered her trunks packed and loaded into a wagon. He'd practically had to throw her over the side of a horse and tie her down to get her to leave. It had only been the threat of wrenching off the precious necklace her mother had gifted her on her twenty-first birthday that kept Calliope in line.

The last gift she'd received. She touched it now, a sapphire rimmed with diamonds that sat perfectly on her throat, the gold chain and clasp delicate enough that it had fallen off a number of times. Sometimes, it simply came loose at just the threat of being wrenched free, as if it had a mind of its own and a desire to escape. Part of the necklace's charm, since she'd felt the same way many times over the years.

"I've no' seen Mary in many years," the old Chief said, his right eye squinting even harder as he gazed at her. "How do I know ye're no' lying?"

"I never lie." Calliope straightened her shoulders. This was true. She never did outright lie. Skirting the truth didn't count.

THE LAIRD'S GUARDIAN ANGEL

"How do I know that's no' a lie?"

Calliope grimaced. "You do not. I suppose it is the first thing a liar would say."

"Aye. So ye admit it?" He tapped the table with a balled-up fist. The same move from her stepsire would have left the cups to topple over, but Chief Ramsey's seemed only to punctuate what he was saying rather than to upset the world order.

"Nay, of course not. I tell the truth. My mother said you were my father, which is why my stepsire brought me here."

"Tossed ye here is more like." The Chief grumbled something under his breath that Calliope was desperate to figure out.

Another of her flaws, she loved a good gossip, and even more so a good insult.

Calliope shrugged, playing nonchalant even though she felt like she might burst from her skin at any moment. Too much had happened in too short a time. Her entire life was upended. But, to his credit, her father had a point. They'd no sooner crossed the border than mean old Edgar—her stepsire—had practically tossed her across it with a finger pointing toward the castle.

"The means by which I arrived are irrelevant. The truth of the matter is I am your daughter. And... my mother is dead." With this last word, her voice caught in her throat, and she had to take a moment's pause before she could figure out what she was going to say next. Though she and her mother were often at odds, and Mary Ramsey's demands on her daughter were weighty, she had loved her.

And now she was dead. That was not a sentence she'd ever presumed to have said. Mary had been so full of life one minute and cold in her bed the next. Not even sick. Not old, despite having a daughter who was old enough to wed.

Calliope had suspicions that her stepsire might have had something to do with her mother's death. A woman in the vitality of her life didn't just fall over one day, never to stand up again. But Edgar had vehemently denied her accusations when he'd told her it was time for her to leave.

"What proof have ye?"

"The word of my mother, your wife, is not proof enough?"

The old Chief snorted. "The word of the English is never enough, lass."

"Funny, my mother said the same thing, only about the Scots."

Chief Ramsey growled, his lip curling up in a snarl. Calliope imagined that on the battlefield, a look like that might have been enough to send his enemies running. She, however, wasn't going anywhere. Rather than run, cower, or duck her head, she sat up taller and stared him straight in the eyes.

"Then why have ye come?" he asked.

She swallowed against the rising emotion, against the anger that made her want to stand and stamp her foot and start swiping the remnants of a meal she'd not been offered to partake in from the table. The one and only time she'd done that in England had earned her boxed ears.

"I have no other place to go. My stepsire removed me from his home. You are my father. Why would I not have come here? And as you recall, I was more dropped on your doorstep than approaching like a customary guest."

That subtle fist popping against the wood drew her attention again. For all his bluster, he wasn't as scary as she thought he might be. "He canna be your stepsire."

Calliope cocked her head. Was that... jealousy? "And yet, that is all I've ever known him as."

Chief Ramsey shook his head and gave her a look that might as well have been a shout: You're daft.

Funny, though, she didn't take offense.

"Mary was my wife and last I checked, I still had a pulse, which means she was still my wife until the day she died, and could no' have remarried, could no' have given ye a stepsire."

Calliope nodded slowly, the same idea having come to her just a few moments before. And it made more sense as to why Edgar felt so compelled to be rid of her. He had no claims on her and certainly wouldn't have wanted to provide the dowry to the English noblemen who had started to court a marriage. Poor Bryce. He probably wondered what had become of her. Perhaps Edgar would say she'd died along with her mother.

"Did you know you had a daughter?" she asked, challenging him to deny her.

"Aye." His fist uncurled, the flat of his palm pressed to the table.

That admission stung. "And you did not see fit to fetch me? Or even visit me?"

"Dinna be offended, lass. I'd no' have crossed the border to lay eyes on ye, and I ordered your mother to send ye north, but she ignored me. The same reason why she left."

"Which was?"

Calliope had a very good idea why, but she still wanted his side of the story. Her mother had made it very clear that Chief Ramsey was cruel and that living on the border holding had been awful and undignified. What lady would want to live in such conditions? Apparently, no amount of complaining made her husband change, and finally, she'd annoyed him so much that he'd tossed her back to England the same way he tossed cabers at festivals.

Ironically, it was the same way Edgar had just tossed Calliope back into Scotland.

To think that throwing trees was deemed a suitable pastime seemed utterly ridiculous. Just as ridiculous as tossing women.

"The trouble between a man and a wife is no one's business but his own." There was a resigned sound to his voice, as though he were very tired, and this an argument he'd had so many times that the very concept of it had been what turned his beard from black to white.

"Well, my mother is gone."

"I am still here."

She drew in a long, weary breath. The man was not going to share what had transpired. Fine. She'd give him the time he needed to adjust to learning his wife was dead, and his daughter was alive. Then she'd figure out a way to get him to tell her. Calliope had learned long ago that an agitated dog wasn't always so willing to approach for a treat, and sometimes you had to toss the meat first.

"I am your daughter, whether you care to admit it or not. If you wish for me to leave, I shall." Calliope pushed away from the unwelcoming table, her feet unsteady, her legs weary from the overlong journey.

"Where will ye go?" The question might have shocked her if he hadn't looked so stricken.

The words themselves appeared callous and uncaring as if he might just pack her bags himself. But the way his brows drew in, his eyes widened, and the ever-so-slightest quiver to his lip belied his indifference.

"I do not know, not that it's any of your concern."

Chief Ramsey stood and walked around the table to where she braced herself on the edge, afraid she'd collapse. She'd be lying to herself if she didn't admit to being slightly terrified by his size.

Ramsey leaned forward, his bushy white brows squeezing

together as he squinted at her, studying her. His gaze fell to the sapphire at her throat, and when he reached out to touch it, though she flinched, she didn't back away.

"Where did ye get that?" His voice had softened even further.

"My mother."

"Did she tell ye where it was from?"

"Aye. My mother said it was a family heirloom."

"She's right. My family."

"Then my family, too." Calliope wanted desperately to ask him who the gem had belonged to, but she needed him to acknowledge that she was indeed his daughter and be done with these silly games. She was exhausted. After a lifetime of trying to conform to her mother's rules, she'd have to figure out her father's terms and then a husband's. Why could she not just be herself and everyone else accept it? Perhaps it wouldn't be so hard if she wasn't so stubborn, so unwieldy.

"'Twas my mother's. I gave it to Mary the day she realized she was with child."

"Pregnant with me," she prodded.

"Nay. A little lad. He died just after he was born. She threw the necklace out the window after that. But, when she grew with child again, I returned it to her. That time was with ... ye."

At last, he'd admitted it. Calliope was his daughter. But even that admission was bittersweet, knowing that she might have had an older brother. Poor sweet baby.

"Did you love her?" Calliope asked.

Ramsey snorted. "'Twas the only reason I was willing to marry an Englishwoman. For love. All the reward it got me. She was a pain in the arse and hated me every day she was here."

Calliope couldn't help but frown. The man did not appear

to be lying. But according to her mother, he'd been a monster, so maybe he was just really good at misleading and manipulation. Except, that didn't match with the man standing before her. Calliope had always had a keen knack for reading people.

"Ye'll stay here." He turned to a woman hovering in the shadows. "Bessie, have a room made up for my daughter."

There were so many questions she wanted to ask, so many she needed clarification on. But exhaustion, both physically and emotionally, was getting the better of her. A week ago, she was the happiest she ever thought she could be. She and her mother had attended court, and there'd been many suitors interested in her hand. It had felt at that moment that she was going to be a happy bride soon, and her mother had promised new fabrics for a trousseau.

Now, she was in Scotland, her mother was dead, and the man she didn't remember as her father was offering her shelter. She stared at him hard, trying to pull from memory some little bit of him, but all she remembered of Scotland was the festival, the groom who'd taught her archery, and the many trees she'd climbed.

How cruel life could be. To present its gifts and hopes and then just as quickly snatch them back.

She pressed her hand to the sapphire again, wondering if it was cursed. A gift given to her mother for the life of a son she'd lost, only to be given to the daughter she'd had and stolen away with.

Aye, indeed, life could be so cruel.

"Go on then. Get some rest. We'll discuss your future more in the morning." Her father patted her arm awkwardly, and Calliope yearned to pull him in for a hug. When was the last time she'd had a hug? Her mother wasn't one for affection, and she'd grown up pretending hugs weren't something she desired.

But now, at this moment, she wanted one very badly.

On feet that felt too weary, Calliope managed to force herself to follow the waiting servant up a winding stone staircase. But instead of being relieved that she'd been accepted into the Ramsey fortress, she felt a little like she was climbing to an uncertain future. But she pushed away the sense of doom that loomed, chalking it up to her overactive imagination.

2

Alistair's shoulder burned like the devil.

A blade cutting through the fabric of his shirt into the thick muscle of his upper arm was nothing compared to what he'd done to his opponent. Battle was brutal, ugly, and necessary. One was either victorious or dead. And truthfully, for him, there wasn't a victory for anyone when it came to battle and death. Only survivors and the dead.

'Twas rare that he was injured in battle, but no warrior ever went unscathed. He wore his scars like badges of honor. The marks on his skin were proof he was alive.

"Ye'll need to get that stitched up." Duncan, his cousin and a warrior in his army, eyed the gash before spitting on the ground. "Bloody bastards."

"Taking a hit is the least I could do for the lad before I ended his life. Though he was a bastard, he died with honor. Unless you consider which side he was fighting on, in which case, we may have to parse out details."

Alistair wiped at the sweat on his brow, then stared down

at the oozing wound on his arm. The battle had been intense, and he did not particularly want to relive it, even if only to discuss their shared victory.

Of course, this was not something he'd ever share with anyone. He was Alistair Bloody Sinclair, Chief of his clan, Baron Roslin, Master of Dunbais Castle. One of three sons born on the same night, brother of Noah, the Earl of Caithness, and Ian, the Earl of Orkney. Elder brother of ladies Matilda and Illiana. Border guardian for Robert the Bruce himself. In other words, Alistair was a force to be reckoned with.

He'd built up a name for himself as one of Scotland's most feared warriors. English army, beware. And he wasn't about to let that reputation be destroyed by something so trivial as his true feelings. What strong man had feelings, anyway?

But his feelings and understanding of war, survival, and protecting his clan also meant he'd never have a wife or a family. How many times had he used a man's loved ones against him? Why the hell would he put his own wife and child through such?

Never.

"How many wounded?" he asked Duncan, forcing himself back to the tasks at hand.

"Only a few. None dead on our side."

Alistair nodded, tearing off his sleeve and tying it around his wounded arm. "Good, because I'd bloody kill them if they were." He laughed if only to lighten the mood and then dismounted from his horse to wash his hands and face in the narrow burn that trickled beside the battlefield. He followed along the edge until he came to a spot that wasn't soaked in blood in order to wash himself off.

"Och, but ye need to have that looked at." This time it

was Broderick standing beside him, eyeing the bleeding gash in his shoulder as Alistair loosened the tie. "What's the point of washing your hands when blood's just dripping down your arm to get it wet again?"

"I'm no' washing away my own blood." Alistair splashed water on his face, giving a good scrub, and then stood, letting out a loud and annoyed groan at the ache in his muscles and the burning in his shoulder. The sound came out more a bellow, causing a few of the vultures who'd come to peck at the dead to scatter.

"I'll get the whisky, my laird." Duncan's words almost made Alistair smile, as though he were resigned to his leader's typical resistance.

Broderick nodded. "I'll get the sewing kit."

Alistair chuckled when they walked away, lucky to have two loyal mates in his charge.

While some of his men worked to clean up the battle—making piles of the bodies to be collected by their loved ones, taking a few good weapons owed to them for the task, lighting fires for a meal, setting up camp—Alistair allowed his wound to be tended by one of his men. Rare was it that he allowed a healer to touch him. Call it superstitious, or maybe it was due to a love affair he'd had with a healer when he was barely twenty.

To say that Alistair had trust issues would be an understatement. Aye, he trusted his men and his brothers, but he always examined anyone else with a critical eye.

"How long are we to wait, Chief?" Broderick threaded the needle and started his mission to close Alistair's wound.

"We wait until we're certain there are no other bands poised to strike." Two times out of three, they were just biding their time. He wasn't going to let anyone get the best of him and his men.

This particular border raid had been by the English, and they were a damned nuisance. From what they'd learned over the last several months was that the bloody *Sassenachs* had developed a strategy to come in waves in hopes that the Scots warriors would have either left the area or be too tired to defend the border.

And unfortunately, Alistair and his men had suffered both. Even now, they were tired, but a warrior's duties never ebbed, and so they rested and waited for the next inevitable wave.

Just like the vultures that circled overhead, waiting their turn for the bodies, the damned *Sassenachs* circled, waiting to peck away at the Scots. Longshanks and his blasted tactics were relentless. Without strong men like Alistair and his army, or a leader like Robert the Bruce, there would have been no telling what might have happened. They'd been fighting this war for as long as Alistair could remember and even further back. Generation after generation had a story to tell.

"I think we should just head them off at the pass," Duncan murmured as he cleaned off his sword. "Why wait like sitting ducks?"

"Because to cross the border would be reckless. It would be seen as Scottish aggression if we ran into the wrong Englishman. We're no' invading another country without the Bruce's explicit orders. We protect from here." However, if Alistair could sneak across the border and put this bloody war to an end, he would.

Duncan frowned but nodded. They had already had this conversation many times before and Alistair was in agreement about them being sitting ducks here with a pile of dead *Sassenachs* on the field, but what could he do? Alistair had to follow orders. Aye, on his own lands he was Chief, but when it came to fighting for the Bruce, the man they wanted to seat on the Scottish throne, Alistair had to follow those orders first. Robert the Bruce would be their king, and before Alistair drew his last breath, they'd see Longshanks and his devil army off Scottish soil for good.

"Trust me, if we've no' seen anyone by sunup we will depart," Alistair said.

"This isn't even our holding," Duncan grumbled under his breath.

"Aye, and our clan will be compensated for providing the swords needed to protect it."

The holding in question was often fought over between the Scots and the English. A fortress to be reckoned with, whoever seized it held the border. The previous baron who kept it safe had perished not a week before, and the man who was his next of kin lived so far north in the Highlands that it would be at least another week or two before he arrived to take his place.

In the meantime, Alistair and his army were here to make sure the English bastards didn't put their flag up on the battlements. Over his dead body.

"I'm no' a caretaker," Alistair said, "but I think we can all agree the extra coin for the good deed of protecting this fortress will do well for our clan. Besides, if we left, the bloody English would cross, and then they'd be on our doorstep. We're here to mitigate the risk. Protect this border in order to protect our own."

The men all nodded in unison. Everyone knew why they were here, even if they were annoyed by the fact. But this was their rotation, and despite being a formidable chief of his own lands, Alistair was also a loyal subject and a supporter of Robert the Bruce. The oath he'd taken was one he'd honor until his last breath. Scotland, the Bruce, his clan, they were all his heart. The only love he would ever have.

"Hand me the whisky." Alistair took that jug they'd brought and held it aloft with his good arm. "Too going home tomorrow." He took a long swallow and passed the jug to Duncan.

"I'll drink to that."

3

"What are ye doing here?" Chief Ramsey stumbled to his feet, the missive he'd been reading falling to the side of the old chair he'd been sitting on.

The wood planks of the worn floor creaked beneath his feet.

For nearly fifteen years, he'd thought his wife was dead, that his daughter had been taken from him too. Having not heard a word, he'd feared the worst. The missive he'd gotten from his wife's cousin after she'd run off had said the two of them passed in a riding accident. All of his worst fears had come true at that moment. A wife gone. His precious daughter joining her wee brother in the heavens. All he'd loved, he'd lost.

Until today.

Fifteen years ago, it had not occurred to Chief Ramsey to question the missive or its contents or the sender. He'd never heard of a cousin named Adam, but he'd been too struck with grief to think otherwise. Too overcome to dare to cross the border. Not that he could have. He would have been killed, and all for naught.

THE LAIRD'S GUARDIAN ANGEL

Except now, come to find out the missive, the cousin, the contents, all fake.

His wife had been alive—and was now dead.

His daughter was alive and upstairs asleep.

And now, standing before him was the man who wanted to take her from him all over again. How might his life have been different if he'd chased after Mary and Calliope when he had the chance?

"You know very well why I'm here." The Englishman rolled his eyes as if speaking to Ramsey was such an annoyance. An effort to remain civil was pointless. The pitch of his vulgar accent grated on Ramsey's ears.

"Explain it to me again." Ramsey indicated the flagon of ale, wishing he'd had the foresight to keep a poisoned goblet on hand just in case. He would have gained great satisfaction from seeing this arsehole writhing on the ground in pain as the last of his breath left his body.

Being near the border of England, it wasn't unusual for him to meet with English noblemen. In fact, he'd agreed to have his men relieve the Sinclair army near the River Tweed in the morning. The first six had already left to relieve them, and he and the rest of his men would follow.

The *Sassenach* standing before him was no different than any of the men he planned to stop at the border come dawn. Well, actually, perhaps there was part of him that was different. He didn't have the squeamish spine that most *Sassenachs* had. Nay, this maggot stood tall and superior as if he had something to gloat about.

"Time to pay the piper." The Englishman nodded to his two cronies, who lurked like blackbirds behind their leader, waiting for the leftovers after he plucked out his prey's eyes.

Well, Ramsey wasn't going to be the prey. Not today. Not ever. And he was damned well going to keep his eyes.

For all the temper he'd hidden from his daughter, he let it unleash now. "Ye'll need to leave, else I flay ye where ye stand."

The Englishman actually chuckled, shaking his head as if Ramsey were just a child. "I plan to, old man, never you fear about that. But first, you'll need to get me what I came for."

"She's not here." Ramsey flexed his fingers, sliding one hand subtly toward the long dagger he kept at his hip. If the man even tried...

English raised a brow, a smirk curling his stupid lips. "Is that a fact? Then why was I told she was?"

"By whom?" Ramsey already knew who, however. That bloody sack of rotting guts had practically run out of the great hall after depositing the girl—well, she was really a woman now, wasn't she?—into the keep. He'd not seen her since she was six years old, and now she was a woman. Though despite the years she'd been gone from him, he recognized the stubborn tilt of her chin, the set of her shoulders. He was grateful that for all of Mary's strict nagging his wife had not been able to erase the spirit from his daughter.

"Let us not pretend that you do not know. It is a game you will lose, and I will grow tired of." English dusted his hands as if wiping away Ramsey, the conversation, the very reason for being here.

The eloquence and bored tone of his unwanted visitor irritated Ramsey. He grimaced, his lips peeling away from his teeth. Back in his day, business was done differently. Men would pick up their weapons, or simply use their fists, and accords would be met by way of beating each other into submission. He might have been a good score older than this welp, but he could take him, he was sure.

Perhaps it was time to bring back some of that age-old wisdom and show the bastard that he meant to change the accord.

He'd only just gotten his daughter back, there was no way in hell he was going to let her go that easily.

Quick as a whip, despite his age, Ramsey drew his dagger.

4

When Calliope was young, the idea of sleeping outside had been an adventure. Even on their race from Scotland to England, all she remembered was the various inns they'd slept in the beds, the excitement of sleeping in a new place. When they'd arrived at Edgar's, the first thing she'd done was jump on her new bed, only to fall off, of course, but that didn't make her stop.

The excitement she'd expected to feel upon laying her head down on this new pillow had yet to come. Rather than excited, Calliope had felt a sense of normalcy—as if this bed were familiar, tugging at loose memories and refusing to lay still.

Where the familiarness of the bed might have allowed one person to close their eyes and fall asleep easily, it only had Calliope tossing and turning and wanting to know how much of her own life she'd missed out on.

The bedchamber was dark, save for a sliver of light shining through the window and the tiny orange of the fire in the hearth. Calliope stared at the differences in light—orange and silver. Did the blood inside her veins, both English and Scottish, clash as much?

They were both light sources, and she was born of two humans. And yet, they were unmatched. And yet, even as she thought it, she realized she didn't know enough about her father to have formed that opinion. Why had her mother left if her father wasn't the evil man she'd portrayed?

Calliope flopped onto her back, an arm over her eyes to hide the light, realizing how utterly ridiculous she was being. Despite her exhaustion, sleep eluded her. The bed was perfectly comfortable, the coverlet warm enough to ward off the chill, and even the sleeping gown laid out for her was adequate.

Nerves must have been the culprit. Sleeping in a new place with new people—although she supposed they weren't new at all, just gone from her memory—and fearing that no one even liked her was not exactly conducive to sleep. The maid, Bessie, who'd shown her to her bedchamber, turned down the bedding and helped her prepare to sleep was cordial but cold. Silent. Rather than ask if Calliope liked the nightgown, she'd held it aloft, nodded, and started stripping her of her dress. Without asking, she'd brushed her hair. Washed her face and then led her to bed, tucking her in without so much as a goodnight.

To be quite honest, it had seemed more like she was the six-year-old she'd been the last time she was here than a grown woman who'd been on the brink of marrying. Calliope searched her mind, trying to remember Bessie. Maybe she'd been the one to tuck her in all those years ago. But her memory came up empty.

The only thing she remembered of sleeping as a young girl was staring at the stars before she succumbed to the night.

Calliope wanted to go back home—to England—to be surrounded by her things and the people who loved her.

She wanted her mother.

She wanted her horse, which she'd been forced to give back to her stepsire upon his leaving. Sweet Serena had turned her head back as she'd been led away, tugged at the reins as if she might come running back to Calliope only to be snapped at by stupid Edgar. The man was so greedy he wasn't even willing to let her have the mare she'd raised and trained herself. Likely, he would sell her off to the highest bidder, and poor, sweet Serena would...

Tears started to leak from her eyes. She was perfectly miserable.

Calliope rolled over in bed, prepared to cry herself to sleep when a strange sound paused her misery. What was that? She sat up a little, cocking her ear toward the door. A subtle *scraaaatch*. Why would a scraping sound give her chills? She chalked it up to servants moving furniture about in the great hall as they swept the floors clean before bed and her overactive imagination that wanted every noise to be an answer to the sense of doom she'd been trying to shove off for the better part of an hour.

The fact that it was so late didn't seem too unusual. Calliope had no idea what kind of time the Ramsey clan kept, and the stories from her mother had made them out to be entirely out of the ordinary, which was putting it mildly. If her mother's retellings were anything to pay attention to, they were a drunken lot who never slept.

Calliope rubbed at her eyes, glad that at least the distraction of the servants cleaning—or imbibing in ale, hard to say—had stopped her tears. The amount of crying she'd done in the last fortnight was sure to leave lasting damage to her eyes, and the puffiness was a new permanent feature. They always stung, and even her vision seemed to be suffering.

The scraping sound continued, and there was perhaps a shout or two. My goodness, they really were as raucous as her mother said. She imagined the servants battling over brooms —or maybe with brooms. Smacking the wooden handles together. Shouting, "En guard," as they whacked at each other over who got to sweep up chicken bones and other discarded remnants.

That part of what her mother had told her appeared to be true. Calliope smiled because she actually wouldn't have minded joining in. She recalled a few broom fights she'd had in the stables before they'd escaped Scotland with sweet Gregor. She'd not seen him upon arriving and wondered if it was possible her father's groom was still in his employ. Although, he'd seemed fairly ancient back then. Though, to be honest, all adults seemed ancient to children. However, the alternative of Gregor not being with them any longer was too much for her to handle, so she determined to bring him breakfast in the morning. Perhaps even to challenge him to a broom fight.

In England, people ate with much more dignified manners. They ate from trenchers, which were portioned out with their meal. They used forks, spoons, and knives. They drank from crystal goblets most nights. And most evenings, her mother would loudly proclaim how happy she was not to be in the land of heathens any longer.

True to her mother's proclamations, when Calliope arrived in her father's hall, they had been eating with their hands and tossing the bones over their shoulders to the waiting and hungry dogs. One warrior spit something onto the ground, and Calliope had been glad they hadn't openly invited her to eat, for she was sure she would have lost everything she'd ingested at that moment. Some of the things her mother said were clearly not an exaggeration.

But now, her stomach growled, and she wished she might have at least swiped a piece of bread to bring back to her new chamber. If she snuck out of her room to the kitchen, there was a chance she might just find a loaf to eat. Then again, she had yet to learn where the kitchen was, if it was even in the castle. Sometimes, they were in an outbuilding. And there was no way she was going outside in the dark. Aye, she was adventurous and mostly brave, but she'd heard plenty about what happened in the dark in Scotland.

And if her mother was right about their eating habits, she was probably right about those habits, too.

The scuffling sounds below grew louder, and she groaned, putting a pillow over her head so she wouldn't have to listen to the noise. Ridiculous, really. Why couldn't they all just go to bed?

She had half a mind to stand up, march to the door, and shout for the love of all things holy that they wrap it up and go to sleep. A loud bang startled her, and she sat up in bed again, the pillow falling to the floor. That was no broom handle clash. For sure, instead of fighting with brooms, they were throwing furniture. *My God, why would they be so ridiculous?*

Enough was enough.

She didn't care that she was new here. She was still the Chief's daughter, and despite her English heritage and the practical strangeness of arriving here, she still deserved respect. And they needed to stop throwing furniture.

Calliope flung back the covers, pulled on a cloak to cover herself, and marched barefoot to the door. Her mother, God rest her soul, would be apoplectic if she saw her now. Ladies simply did not leave their rooms undressed and without shoes. How many times had her mother told her that? At least a thousand.

But ladies were not also typically without sleep for days traveling across the border in mourning either. And indeed, they were not subjected to this kind of racket.

She reached for the door handle, the sounds of the bluster below the stairs getting louder and louder, which only fueled her need to let them know their rudeness would not be tolerated. Tourneys were meant to be held outside, not in great halls.

Just as she opened the door, it was pushed in on her, and she stumbled backward but did not fall.

Bessie stood there, frantic in appearance. Eyes wide, hair a mess. Calliope blinked, sure her eyes were deceiving her.

"My lady. The castle is under attack." Bessie looked harried and scared in the moonlight—and she also appeared to be telling the truth. "Ye must bar your door. Orders from your father."

Calliope straightened, the rebellious side of her suddenly rearing its head. "What? Attacked by whom?"

"I dinna know, my lady. Please, bar your door. And here." Bessie thrust a blade at her. "For your protection, should they..."

"Should they what?" But the question was moot. She knew precisely what Bessie meant. Should the enemy break down the barrier of her door. Should the enemy decide, she was ripe for the taking.

She'd stab the ever-loving hell out of them.

Calliope blinked at the small knife in the housekeeper's hand. "What about you, Bessie? Have you a knife?"

"Aye. I'll be fine. Take it." Bessie pressed the handle of the knife against Calliope's palm, which she hadn't realized she'd even held out. And then Bessie was gone, shutting the door firmly with the expectation that Calliope would listen and bar it against the intruders. Which she should do, of course.

Her mother had been right. The savage Scots were attacked all the time. She'd not even been here a day, and already there was a battle. No wonder her mother had gone back to the safety of England, where Calliope belonged.

She put the bar on the door, wiggling it and trying to open it just to make sure it was secure. Her heart pounded behind her ribs, as wood pounded beneath her feet. She'd never been under attack before. The most fighting she'd ever witnessed had been at a festival. And even those battles could be so brutal she had to turn away.

The blade shook in her hand, and she put it on the mattress, not feeling comfortable enough to carry it the way her fingers trembled. A bow and arrow she was comfortable with. A dagger? Not as much. But that didn't mean she wouldn't use it if necessary. Taking a life to save her own was not something she'd ever had to do, but it was something she'd known she had permission to do if necessary.

From the recesses of her mind, a voice spoke, a memory evoked of her father telling her, "Calliope, never let a bastard try to steal the beat of your heart. Stab them where it hurts." If her mother had overheard that, it probably was part of the reason she'd fled. Lady Mary wouldn't abide a daughter knowing how to kill.

Except, Calliope did know.

So many questions rambled through her mind. Such as, did attacks last long? Would they simply leave when they were finished? And what in blazes could they want?

Was she going to have to kill a man tonight?

She rushed to the window, peeling back the fur blocking the night chill, and stared into the oddly quiet courtyard.

Aye, calm, but seeing no one there didn't appease her mind, in fact, it only made her more fearful. When she'd arrived with Edgar, the courtyard had been full of people and warriors.

Of course, the people would be asleep, but didn't the warriors stand on duty?

Her gaze roved over the battlement walls. No one, or wait... a few someones, but they no longer stood. Otherwise, they were discarded sacks of grain covered in warrior garb. But she wasn't so naïve and stupid as to believe that. Someone had felled the men on the Ramsey battlements.

Beyond the wall, she squinted into the night, trying to make out if an army stood just out of sight, but she could only see the trees in the distance. Whoever had come to attack the castle had left no trace of themselves outside the wall. Either that, or they were as sneaky as wraiths, and she couldn't make them out.

Below stairs, what she'd thought was the scuffle of broomsticks and tossing furniture shifted into shouts and the clang of metal. If she'd only listened hard enough, she would have known the difference.

Swords clashing. Weapons cracking into bone. Bodies behind tossed.

A shiver raced over her spine, and Calliope, for the first time, realized the actual danger she was in. Aye, her hands had started to tremble when a blade was thrust into them, but she'd been so overcome with questions she hadn't taken a moment to truly realize she was in danger. Aye, she'd barred the door, but that had just been following the instructions of the maid.

Oh, dear, heavens, Bessie!

Calliope couldn't just let her go off toward danger. Didn't she want to be behind a barred door as well?

Boots. She needed her boots. Perhaps there was a reason her mother had instilled in her the necessary habit of always wearing shoes.

The better to keep your toes from stepping on a rock. Her mother's words echoed in her mind from when she'd been young and balked. But now she understood why it was necessary. How many times had her own mother, under Ramsey's protection, had to run from her bedchamber when they were under attack?

Without hose, Calliope thrust her feet into her boots and made quick work of lacing them up. She tossed on her gown, hastily lacing and buttoning that as well, not at all caring for the lopsided indication that she'd missed an eyelet. There was no time to fix it, and really, her gown was the last thing on her mind.

She might be new here, but Calliope was still a Ramsey, and Ramseys didn't back down from danger.

Or at least that was what her mother had told her—though she certainly hadn't meant the women.

5

They'd woken at first light after only sleeping with one eye shut.

Without a sign of the enemy, Alistair and his men packed up camp and quietly left as though they'd never arrived, leaving the watch to the next band of warriors commissioned by the Bruce, whom they'd already briefed on the skirmish from the previous day.

Six Ramseys, with the rest to follow. Apparently, there'd been an unexpected delay.

"I'm no' sure we should leave ye alone," Alistair said.

"Never ye fear, Sinclair. Our Chieftain is right behind us."

Alistair had an uneasy feeling about this. Never before had Ramsey sent men to relieve him. He decided to be nosy. "What was the expected delay?"

"Family matters. Clan business."

Alistair grunted, not particularly caring for that answer. Ramsey's family was his clan; his wife absconded with his daughter over a decade ago, and both of them perished in a terrible accident.

"Anything I can help with?" he offered. It was always a

good idea to help the clans that surrounded his own. The strength of their borders depended on it.

"Nay. Chief Ramsey will get it sorted and be out shortly. Ye all go off now. The English willna bother us before he arrives."

"We both know that's not especially true."

"Let it be so today."

Alistair narrowed his eyes. Ramsey's men were certainly cocky. But there was some truth to what they were saying as well. His own scouts had reported all was quiet this morning. There didn't appear to be an imminent attack on the horizon, and if Ramsey and the rest of the reinforcements would be there soon, then who was Alistair to remain? He'd only appear as if he didn't trust the Ramseys, and he didn't want to send that message. They were allies. And trust was everything. Their word was their bond.

Alistair would be lying if he didn't say he felt like the castle on the River Tweed was like a wee lad being fostered out from clan to clan to learn the ways of a warrior. The only difference was the big stone walls would never learn to pick up a sword. Nor to take care of itself.

His shoulder burned where it had been stitched, and his fingers tingled, indicating the damage to more than just skin and muscle. Alistair squeezed his hand into a fist around the blade he kept in his boot to ensure he could still handle it. Satisfied that the tingling didn't mean he would lose the ability to wield a weapon, he shoved the knife back into his boot. One of the elders of his clan had lost the use of his hand in a similar injury, being forced to retire from the fight well before his time. The only satisfaction he'd had was sitting at the head of the table on Alistair's council. Augie was a godsend, to be sure, with sound advice Alistair had used often.

They'd be home in three days, but even then, he could not rest. He'd have to write missives and report what happened here to the Bruce and then to his brothers Ian and Noah, who held two other points in the Highlands—Caithness and Orkney—

sound against the English. Well, English enemies. Both his brothers had crossed the border when it came to marrying. Not that they'd planned to wed English ladies. But ironically, they both had. Fortunately, Alistair's sisters-by-marriage were heartier than some Scots he knew and just as feisty as his brothers deserved. In fact, he got quite a laugh out of the hell they raised.

"We'll leave ye to it. God be with ye," Alistair said.

"With the devil by his side," jested the Ramsey warrior. The exact exchange they had each time.

Alistair gave his men the signal to mount up. The next three days would be long, and he just wanted to be home and sleep in his own bed for at least a night or two. They had to cross through Ramsey lands to get back to Dunbais. They'd probably see Chief Ramsey on the way, and he could relay that the transition went well. Or perhaps they'd have a wee skirmish. One never really knew.

Chief Ramsey was a mean son-of-a-bitch. Sometimes, he sent his men out to spar with Alistair and his warriors just for the hell of it. As if to remind them they were crossing territory ruled over by a powerful man. Or mayhap to just keep them on their toes.

The thing was, the Sinclairs never really took him seriously.

Aye, Ramsey's warriors could be fearsome, but they weren't as well-trained as Alistair's men. And the Chief was half-crazed since his wife had run away to England with their only child fifteen years before.

Rumor had it he'd tried to take a dozen women to bed to beget another heir, only for their wombs to come up empty. It would seem God was punishing him for having scared off his wife. Then again, Alistair recalled meeting the woman as a lad, and she'd scared the hell out of him. He'd always harbored some thoughts that Chief Ramsey had gotten the better end of the deal there.

The irony was not lost on Alistair.

Though he did not always like the man, Alistair did respect Chief Ramsey. The man's lands bordered his own, and so he made sure to be respectful as they crossed. Diplomacy was important between the clans that bordered him. Especially since he and his men had to make these treks to the border every three months to serve the Bruce at the castle on the River Tweed, with the Ramseys following.

It'd been nearly a month since he'd been home, and he longed for the sweetness of his cook's bread and honey and an excellent cold ale by his hearth. Just thinking about it made his mouth start to water. Warm bread, cold ale. Heaven on earth.

There'd be a day of catching up on his correspondence, meeting with his tenants, and getting updates on what had happened while he was gone. He'd make the rounds of his lands and try to speak to each person to see how they fared and how he could help. He'd host a day of trials if necessary, open his great hall for a feast, all welcome. And then it would be back to training his men until three months went by, and he was back at the border, staring across the River Tweed and waiting for the English bastards to dare to cross.

Their horses' hooves barely made a sound as they galloped down the road, softened by the night's dew.

His men were eager to get home, too. The further they were from the border, the better everyone would feel. There was relief in the distance most of the time, but his brothers had seen the English even as far north as they were in Scotland. No land was sacred to Longshanks's men.

Still, they would rest safe for at least a day or two, knowing that they'd either passed zero English on the way or that they'd eradicated those who dared to taint their lands.

Once they got to Sinclair lands, the routine was always the same. Duncan would disappear into his croft with his wife, and Broderick would likely cozy up with one of the many widows who clambered over themselves to lie with him.

Alistair's bed would be cold, but that cold was a comfort to him. The silence at night was what he looked forward to the most. A chance to breathe. A chance to regroup. And with this damned shoulder injury, a chance to heal.

They crossed into Ramsey lands just after the sun reached its peak, melting the frozen dew from the grass and causing it to drip on their heads from the trees.

Alistair stared at the road ahead, his eyes narrowing as he took in the state of the thoroughfare. Disturbed by dozens of footprints and hoof prints. Aye, this was the road the Ramseys took to get here, but there were only six on horseback, and this marring of the dirt did not match.

Raising his arm, he indicated for his men to stop and then dismounted, crouching near the ground, to examine the disturbances in the dirt. He ran a finger along the outline of a footprint.

"Recent," he muttered, rubbing the dirt between his thumb and forefinger.

Duncan and Broderick joined him. The latter traced the outline of a boot print, making note of the point near the toe with a tap of his finger.

"I'd say no' older than a day, if no' less."

"And," Alistair, too, examined the boot print, different

from their own in the angles. But more telling was the distinct "ER" pressed into the mud in the ring of a horse's shoe. Edward Rex. King Edward I of England. Also known as Longshanks. His men had been here. "I'd say English."

"How did we miss them?" Duncan growled, standing and whirling around as if he expected a band of English to leap from the trees.

"They went round our us, knew what our perimeter was," Broderick said.

"The English are no' normally so sneaky," Duncan remarked.

"They had a purpose." Alistair immediately thought of Dunbais Castle. Could his holding be their purpose? The battle was often brought to his doorstep, given his position as border guardian. Longshanks had allegedly had his men hang wanted signs of him in local taverns. Of course, the locals laughed and tore them down. The likeness to himself was apparently comical, though Alistair had never seen one of the signs.

Still, he didn't like what he saw, and the sense of unease he'd felt at the border only grew. "We need to hurry."

They remounted, all of them ill at ease now, their eyes scanning for any subtle signs of an ambush.

"Keep your eyes and ears open for anything out of the ordinary. There's no telling how close we are to the band that's passed through here."

His men nodded.

They galloped down the road, keeping their gazes on the surrounding forest that lined either side, listening for the sounds of the enemy. They stopped in a clearing that looked to be where a camp had been made, the vague scents of a fire recently put out still lingering in the air. Even the grass where they'd sat or slept was still flattened.

Alistair found the makeshift firepit, kicking at the ashes and bits of burnt wood. There was nothing left behind to indicate who the interlopers were, but more of the same boot prints and those same "ER" prancing about as if to mock them.

Down the road, they encountered another scuffle in the dirt, only this time, it wasn't as pronounced as before—as if there were only a few riders involved.

"What the devil," Alistair grumbled as he jumped off his horse and bent to examine several footprints that were notably smaller in width and length. "This is a woman's footprint."

"What would a woman be doing with the English?"

"I'm no' even sure they are of the same party," Alistair said, glancing up and staring down the road as if his desire to see who had passed through here would be enough to conjure them from thin air.

"Were they being followed?" Duncan posed.

"I dinna know. But there is something off."

"Mayhap Ramsey's wife has come back to him," Broderick said with a shrug that wasn't too convincing.

"Is she still alive?" Duncan asked. "I heard he fed her to his dogs."

Alistair rolled his eyes. "The woman ran back to England like her cowardly heart demanded that she do. Then she died in an accident."

"I dinna see any woman coming back to the Ramsey, he's meaner than a snake. Then again, if she did die, maybe she's come back to haunt him," Broderick said.

"An English woman's ghost come all this way," Duncan chuckled. "Poor old bastard."

Alistair rolled his eyes. "No' his wife, nor her ghost."

And yet, there, for all of them to see, were the very tiny

prints that could have only been made by a woman's shoe, mixed in with the horseshoes labeled "ER."

"There is a chance it's a man's shoe. Or a lad's." Duncan offered with a shake of his head.

"A small chance," Alistair conceded. He touched a print, pinched the dirt in his fingers, and brought it to his nose. There was just the faintest scent of flowers. Likely not from the shoe's owner but the patches of wildflowers that grew all around him. But still... "However, I'm thinking 'tis a woman."

"Are ye wanting to stop by Ramsey's keep to find out who?" Broderick laughed. "I think it worth the fight, just to appease our curiosity."

Alistair grinned. "It could be fun to do so. The man would likely demand satisfaction for our intrusion. But we'd know if Lady Ramsey had returned from the dead."

"Concerned neighbors," Duncan said.

"Aye, we're so verra concerned." Broderick gave an exaggerated nod.

"Ramsey," Alistair playacted, "Have ye got a woman in there?"

The men laughed as they remounted their horses. But as soon as they started to ride over the tracks of dozens of English soldiers, their mood returned somber once more. Alistair worried that whoever the woman was, she was not safe on the road or wherever she was headed with the English out there, too.

6

The chill racing up and down her spine, the hairs standing on end on her neck, warning her to remain in her bedchamber and bar the door as she'd been instructed to do, were lost on Calliope at the moment.

Well, perhaps not lost so much as ignored.

Aye, self-preservation warred with her instinct to protect what was hers. And though she barely remembered this keep or its people, she was the only daughter and heir of Ramsey. If the castle was under attack, was she not duty-bound to protect it?

Wouldn't that be what her father expected? However, it was also her father who bid her bar the door. But that was because he didn't know her very well. He thought her weak, perhaps. But there wasn't a weak bone in Calliope's body. Except when it came to berry tarts—then she was very weak indeed.

The hinges creaked on her door as she slowly eased it open. She winced at the sound, praying that it had not alerted any lurking enemies to her presence. Holding her breath, she waited a split second in case there was some ghastly enemy about to leap from behind somewhere to stab her into oblivion.

No one did. And so, Calliope stepped out into the corridor, certain she could feel the chill of the stone through the soles of her shoes, and knowing at the same time that was impossible.

What was she doing? This was stupid, one side of her brain warned, while the other side encouraged her to creep forward. To hold that dagger high and bring it down on their attacker's head.

But yet again, she paused. What was her dagger when armed warriors had swords longer than her arm in a fight?

She turned around, ready to return to her room, when a bellow of outrage from below practically shook the walls. Calliope whirled back toward the stairs. There was no going back.

Her boots made no sound as she gingerly pressed her feet into the corridor's stone, one foot in front of the other. Her dagger was clutched tightly in her hand, and her skirts were lifted in the other so she didn't catch a toe on the hem and take a tumble.

The sounds of the fight below the stairs grew louder the closer she drew to the circular stairs. Once at the top, sweat beaded on her brow, and her stomach had tightened so fiercely she thought there was a very good chance she was going to throw up.

Calliope gritted her teeth, swallowing the bile rising in her throat and demanding she get a hold of herself. She was a Ramsey, by God. And she needed to start acting like one.

She put one foot down on the step, then another, leaning her shoulder into the stone wall to hold herself up as she went. Go back, go back, one part of her brain said. No, you must protect what is yours, the other side replied.

Barely down eight steps, barely rounding a corner, the grunts, groans, and clashes of metal echoed in her ears as though she were in the thick of the battle that raged just out of sight. Calliope winced, then straightened. This was not a time for wincing. This was not a time for her to suddenly get a fit of the vapors, not that she was prone to them. This was the time to help her father.

Down five more stairs. A closed door on Calliope's right. She pressed her ear to it, wondering if this was the great hall, but also knowing instinctively it was not; the great hall had been wide open to the stairs. There was silence on the other end of this door. Not where the fight was currently taking place. Perhaps this was her father's bedchamber or his study.

She couldn't remember how many floors she'd climbed when she'd followed the maid to her bedchamber the night before. Exhaustion had been so deep, and only fear rushing through her body now kept her upright.

But it hadn't been many. Perhaps one more time down around, and then Calliope would be in full view of the great hall with its long, lonely table and great hearth that could fit an entire family of three generations inside it. The image conjured in her mind was her father sitting at the other end. And the fear that raged after was that she'd never see him sitting there again.

Not three steps down, her shoulder still pressed to the stone, her face close to the mortar, there was a smear of blood. So close to her face, she could smell the metallic scent of it. If there was blood here, then that meant the room she'd just passed must have had some sort of battle? Or perhaps the battle had started right here where she stood and raged downward. She tried hard not to think what she might have found behind that closed door.

This was ludicrous. Calliope was out of her mind. This smear of blood and the sounds raging all around her were signs enough that she should return to the safety of her room. She was brave. She was a Ramsey. She could protect herself—maybe—against an assailant. But an attacking army? What could she do to help herself and her clan? The answer was nothing.

Until this moment, when she'd not been faced with the actual realness, dangerousness, and seriousness of her situation, the fear of what might come seemed almost to be on the outside of her periphery. Happening to someone else, she was just going to bear witness to it. And now...

Now she was looking at a very real, very recent, stain of blood on the stones of her father's castle.

Calliope's knees trembled, one of them buckling, and she quickly sank to her bottom on the steps before she fell completely, which would both cause her physical harm and alert the enemy to her presence. Both of which had the same ending result—physical pain or death.

Then again, if she just sat here like a weakling, they would come charging up the stairs anyway to get her, and then where would she be? Slaughtered.

She shuddered, remembering her mother's warnings of the fighting between the clans and the terrible ways they lived. That was not a fate she wanted any part of. For all the bravery she'd tried to muster in the past few minutes, this was not the way she wanted her life to end.

She should be in England, dancing at court, flirting. Not holding someone else's dagger with blood a foot from her face.

This meant she should cease her descent into mayhem.

What she really needed to do was escape the castle and find help for her father.

But who would help her, and how would she even know where to go? There would be neighboring clans, but what if those bordering Ramsey lands were the ones who were invading now? What if her father had no allies?

She racked her brain for anything her mother might have told her that could help her now. The only thing she could remember was something about the Sinclairs. The last festival they'd gone to, the Sinclair warriors had won every contest. Her mother had remarked on how every one of them had been handsome as well as incredibly fearsome. In fact, that night, she'd also overheard her mother say she'd never seen men such as the Sinclairs who exuded such strength while also being beautiful. But that was fifteen years ago. They could all be dead. And they were most certainly old.

Yet her mind was telling her to go to the Sinclairs. As if her mother had reached out from beyond the grave to pluck this memory from thin air and plant it in her head.

Calliope forced herself to stand, her fingertips brushing the blood on the stone as she did. She shuddered, wondering who had bled here as she wiped the remnants on her skirt. She needed to find a way out of the castle and to the Sinclairs. A feat that would prove much more difficult than she had time to contemplate, considering she didn't even know what direction to go.

Her father's booming voice below gave her pause just as she'd planned to return to the floor her chamber was on to locate a servants' stair. She glanced over her shoulder, hesitating even as she trembled.

"Why have ye come, *Sassenach*?" Anger laced her father's voice so deep that she barely recognized him.

Sassenach? Who was that? She'd have to remember the

name so she could relay it to the Sinclairs—if she made it out of here alive.

There was a snort of a response as if her father's question was preposterous.

"Answer me. I'll know why ye've killed me."

Killed? Calliope's free hand went to her throat, and she squeezed to keep the whimper of fear from escaping. Her father couldn't die. Not now! She'd only just returned. Wanted desperately to know who he was. What a cruel world it was that Fate would kill both her parents in the same month.

She clutched the dagger tighter, wishing she could charge into the great hall to save him. And knowing at the same time that if she did so, there would be two dead bodies on the floor. The last of her father's direct line. She couldn't do that. Not when he had ordered her to remain above the stairs. She didn't want him to die, knowing she'd died too.

"The lot of you heathens will be wiped from the earth. Our English king will see to it." The venom in the other man's voice was palpable. And he wasn't Scottish. That part was extremely obvious and concerning. Did the man who was trying to kill her father know her mother? Know Edgar?

"Not my king," her father growled.

"Your denial is precisely the reason. We will take this border holding, and we will take the next one and the next, and all of you, every single one of you, who dares to try and keep us from it, will suffer the same sentence. And I will personally take your daughter to my bed."

Her father made a strangled noise of rebellion, and her heart seized in her chest.

"Execution, by order of King Edward of England," the Englishman named Sassenach shouted, the words sending razors of fear cutting through her nerves.

"Ye and your bloody king can rot in hell!" her father bellowed, but there was a wobble beneath the shout that sent a ripple of fear coursing through Calliope.

Her father was weakening. Whatever the man had done to him had well and truly been enough of a blow to see that his Fate was sealed. He had killed him. Maybe even before she'd come down. Some wounds took their time in draining life's essence from a man.

Chief Ramsey—her father—was going to die.

Which meant she was to be the new Chieftain to the Ramsey clan. In England, they would laugh at such a notion. A woman in charge? Not likely. But here in Scotland, lines were passed from man to woman to man and back again as long as they were the first in line. And though she wasn't the first in line—that had been her wee baby brother's position—she was the one who was alive.

Calliope bit her tongue as another whimper rose up her throat.

There was a laugh now coming from *Sassenach*, the sound gritty and vile as if he were enjoying this moment. Celebrating her father's death, his murder.

"Know that you and your people will die here with you, and this time tomorrow, the English will roam these halls, rule this land, and all that you have worked for, desired, will be dust to the wind like your old, failing body." There was a spitting sound that sent rage coursing through her.

"This body is no' a failure yet." There was a grunt, two, three, and then a bellow of pain. Her father had clearly mustered some last bit of resistance left in his body. And though her mind knew the bellow of pain had not been the Englishman's, her heart hoped it was.

"Die, old man." The silence was deafening.

Calliope let out a small whimper this time as her mind

brought forth images of what could be happening. Her father got a second wind to fight the enemy. Getting in a hit, then another, before a final death blow was meted out by *Sassenach*.

"What was that? Who is there?" The man's voice sounded searching, and she realized too late it was her own sound that he was speaking of.

Not today. Calliope was not going to die today.

"Go and see." *Sassenach* gave the order, leaving no doubt as to what had just happened. Wiping away any last vestiges of hope that perhaps her father had rallied enough to kill the Englishman instead.

Why were the English here anyway? Edgar had been hurried in his desire to rush off. Was it because he knew this man was coming? She prayed that hadn't been the reason behind it. The reason he'd left her here was to die. Edgar had been her stepsire for most of her life. She'd thought he'd loved her as a daughter. But it had all been for show.

The man's words came rushing back. It was a proclamation of what King Edward hoped to accomplish in Scotland by eradicating the people who lived here and belonged here.

Had Edgar betrayed her and her mother?

But there was no time for her to speculate. Footsteps pounded across the great hall and then sounded on the stairs, and she forced herself to turn and flee back up the stairs from where she'd come.

7

They surrounded the *Sassenach*, their swords outstretched toward his neck and those of his companions. Alistair grinned, ignoring the pain in his shoulder as he eyed the band of men they'd been following up and down.

The weaklings were shaking in their English boots, a few of them looked very close to pissing themselves, and one of them definitely already had. Cowards.

"What are ye doing on Ramsey land?" Alistair demanded. The ache in his shoulder made him surlier, and where he might have tried to be nicer to coax what he wanted out of the fools who dared traipse across the border, the pain at the hands of one of their countrymen left little compassion if any inside him.

Och, who was he kidding? He'd never be nice to an Englishman. He hated the bloody lot of them. In fact, they were lucky to be alive. Before he'd met his sisters-by-marriage, he would have killed any Englishman on sight. He only gave pause now in case they were related. Which he doubted very much. Rhiannon and Douglass would give him much praise for his restraint, he was certain. And to be honest, he loved their praise.

"We come in peace," the man who was clearly their leader said, his hands held upright in surrender. Though his voice held no hint of worry, the way he was squinting his eyes said otherwise. It was a good sign then.

"Did you hear me? We. Come. In. Peace." The leader's tone sounded as if he wasn't sure they spoke English, pronouncing each syllable loudly and slowly.

Alistair frowned, exchanging a glance with Duncan and Broderick. Was the *Sassenach* drunk? There was no way he'd come in peace, and certainly not a way in which Alistair would believe a dammed word out of his mouth. The man was daft if he thought they would. He was also daft for thinking they didn't speak English.

Unable to help himself, Alistair laughed. "Peace ye say? Was it peace that had us fighting your countrymen yesterday? Peace that has us patrolling the borders so ye willna come across to rape our women and steal our livelihoods? Or was it peace that had your king determining that men of your ilk could take our brides on their wedding nights to try and impregnate them?" Alistair shook his head, a cruel smile forming on his lips. "I dinna think peace is the word ye meant, ye maggot."

"Maggot?" The man had the audacity to bluster as if he'd had his feelings hurt at Alistair's insult. His cheeks turned red, and the hands he'd held up in surrender a moment ago turned to fists. "I am no maggot, and you, well, you are a heathen."

Alistair's grin widened. "Och, that's more like it. No more talk of peace, ye insult us both by even saying the word. Let me hear ye tell it how much of a heathen I am so I have reason to finish this business and kill ye and your men. I grow weary, and I'm in need of a good ale."

The man took a threatening step forward, only to be stopped by the tip of Duncan's sword against his chest. "You would not dare!"

Alistair laughed again, and this time, Duncan, Broderick, and the rest of their men joined in. A dozen Scots laughing in his face only made the man's face turn nearly purple.

"Dare?" Alistair asked. "I believe that's my middle name. Enough dallying, I'd like to see ye bleed."

"Peace is the right word," the man blustered, a stamp of his foot as if he were a child in a grown man's body. "I was delivering my late wife's daughter."

Alistair narrowed his eyes. "She died in childbirth? And what sort of man brings his wife to Scotland and delivers the bairn himself?" Heaven help him, but Alistair would never understand the bloody English. What a fok—

"My wife did not die in childbirth." The man shifted on his feet, seeming agitated now. There was something about the way that he spoke that seemed untrustworthy.

Alistair narrowed his eyes. "Och, so ye killed her then?"

The *Sassenach* blanched white, even his lips thinned to colorless lines. His mouth popped open and shut like a fish out of water. The men around him stared like they hadn't thought of that possibility until now. Interesting. What exactly had Alistair stumbled upon. The woman's footprints. Did they belong to his wife? Was she now dead? Was he planning to frame the Scots for her death?

"So ye did kill her," Alistair said, clear from the way he was acting that was the case.

"Nay!" the man shouted. "I did no such thing."

Alistair cocked his head. "Ye're no' making sense. And ye look guilty."

"The only thing I'm guilty of is leaving her daughter in this godforsaken land."

Alistair imagined a bairn left out in the wild for anything to pick at her. The poor wee thing. He heard no cries. Either she was far from here, or she'd already been taken by a beast or the fairies, and a changeling would come in her place. Either way, this man was a cruel and heartless bastard who deserved the Fate that Alistair was about to provide him with.

"I assure ye, we've God aplenty here," Alistair said. "Now, say your prayers loudly so he might hear them over the whining from your mouth. It seems God has put ye in our path for us to mete out your punishment for murdering your wife and bairn."

"For the love of..." The man growled under his breath, and it was all Alistair could do to contain himself and not dispatch him right then and there. "My wife's daughter is a grown woman. She is half Scots, and I returned her to where she belongs."

His wife's daughter. Was she not his then?

"Half Scots, ye say?" Now Alistair's attention was well and truly grabbed. Perhaps the tiny footprints they'd seen belonged to this young woman, not his wife? Curious. "Who did ye leave her with?"

"The Ramseys." The man sneered up at him as if that was supposed to be an insult.

Despite their skirmishes over the years, the Ramseys were their allies, especially against the English. If he was insulting the Ramseys, then he was insulting the Sinclairs.

"Why did ye no' keep her for yourself?" Alistair was more curious than anything to know why the fool *Sassenach* would have risked crossing the border to drop a wee thing in

Ramsey lands. A grown woman or not, she had tiny feet. Made no sense.

"Keep her? You heathens are all the same. Why would I do such a thing? I loved her mother, not her, and I would never take her to wife. She's too... stubborn. And she's bloody Scots."

"And her mother was no'?"

"No. Mary was full English."

Interesting. This English bastard claimed to have loved her, and yet it was obvious he killed her, too. Perhaps it was good then that he'd brought her daughter to Scotland, returning her to her father so she would be safe. Clearly, she was not in this man's hands.

"Ramsey's daughter, then?" Everyone knew that Ramsey had gotten himself an English bride during a border raid. She'd been around for a time and then left. Rumors spread rampantly through Scotland as to why, but anyone who knew the old bastard just assumed Lady Mary had grown tired of him and run off. Hell, if she'd been a relation of his, he'd have encouraged her to run off. Then came the news she'd been killed. No word until now. How odd.

Then again, this man had said wife. She couldn't be his wife if she was Ramsey's wife. Alistair was an intelligent man, but this situation was a bit much to parse out. He simply shook his head at the fool man.

"Answer me, *Sassenach*. Was it Ramsey's daughter?"

"I owe you nothing." Stubborn as they came, the man lifted his thin chin.

"That's true, ye dinna. But, perhaps I'll show ye mercy."

Duncan shifted his head, a look of concern etched on his brown. Alistair never showed mercy to the English. Especially not when they were this annoying.

"A quick death for ye and your comrades."

"Ha! You think I'm going to divulge information in exchange for a quick death. You really are stupider than our king told us you were."

Alistair shrugged. "'Tis up to ye, but I'll have ye know, my man right there," he nodded his head toward Duncan, "loves to watch a man die slowly. First, he'll take your fingernails. Then, your fingers. Then your wrists, then to your elbows and shoulders. Chopping until your limbs are in a hundred bloody chunks, but still, ye remain alive."

Duncan grinned wildly, nodding like a hungry beast. He would, of course, do no such thing, but the terror on the *Sassenach's* face was priceless.

Another stamp of his foot, his hands in the air. "All right, all right, I'll tell you! Just don't chop me up."

"I accept your plea for mercy. Do go on." Alistair stabbed his sword into the ground and crossed his arms over his chest to listen.

"She is Ramsey's daughter. I was her mother's lover, though we called each other husband and wife. The old man wouldn't give her a divorce even when she begged him. But he denied her. She faked her own death. Only now, she is actually dead. An accident."

"I'm surprised he let her go at all," Alistair said.

"Why?" the Englishman shrugged. She hated him; forcing her to remain would only be an embarrassment."

Alistair laughed. "Ye dinna know the Scots verra well then."

"And a good thing. I'd not want to know any of you, and I'm only here out of obligation to my former wife."

"Lover," Alistair corrected. He may not have liked Ramsey, but he wouldn't disrespect him by letting another man call his wife his own.

The man narrowed his eyes, and again, Alistair wondered at his hesitation in just running him through.

"I... humbly beg of you that you allow me to pass. Understand that I did Ramsey a favor in bringing his only daughter back. Would you kill the man who returned her to him?"

The only words the man had said thus far that made any sense at all. Alistair made a disappointed noise in the back of his throat. A good point, he had, and not one that Alistair could find fault with. Ramsey was likely very happy to have his heir back, even if she was a lass. Though having grown up in England with a traitorous mother, and this maggot as her stepsire could not have made her into a strong woman. She would likely be a disappointment.

Still, if Ramsey had let the man go, then it wasn't Alistair's right to kill him. He wouldn't ruin their alliance by doing so.

He indicated that his men should lower their swords. Duncan was the loudest in his disappointment, groaning and stabbing at the earth, which had several of the Englishmen jumping.

"While I would have very much enjoyed watching the lot of ye bleed out, it is no' my place to issue such punishment. Clearly Ramsey saw a reason to keep ye alive. Be gone from here. If I happen across ye again, I will no' hesitate to see my lust for blood sated."

The *Sassenach* gasped, not so much in shock as he was sucking in air through lungs that had been deprived of oxygen for far too long. Still, he wavered. What the hell?

"Be gone with ye, I said." Alistair shot his arm to the side, waving then on, and Duncan helped him out by slapping the flank of the man's horse, which took off at a gallop without his rider.

The Englishman stole one of his entourage's mounts and

gave chase, the rest following at a pace that was likely to drain their horses' energy quite soon. Idiots.

Alistair turned back to his men, a look of disgust on his face. "Why the hell would Ramsey let that man live? He's been foking his wife all these years and claiming ownership? Being a father to his daughter?" Alistair shook his head. "No wife of mine, nor her lover, would survive such."

"Does that mean ye've changed your mind about finding a wife?" Duncan asked the tone of his voice a challenge as well as a tease.

"No' on your life. My lands will go to my brothers' sons, whoever has one first."

"A bloody shame, my laird. For ye'd make some woman—"

Before his man could finish, Alistair punched him in the shoulder. "Do shut up. Let's ride. I want to stop by the Ramsey keep to make certain we didna just let an enemy of Scotland go."

8

As quietly as she could, Calliope ran from door to door on the castle's upper level, checking handles and looking for a way out. For all she knew at this point, even the poor maid who'd bid her to bar her door had perished at the hands of whoever was below stairs. Whoever was giving chase.

Murderer.

Her eyes blurred with tears, and her heart was pounding so forcefully against her chest that it was bound to alert the enemy to her presence. As if the pounding of her heart, cracking against her ribs, was somehow sending out a pulse against the stone walls.

She just needed to get out of here before it was too late. Every second that she didn't find escape was a second they were closer to her.

At last, at the end of the corridor, there was a small door, and when she opened it, narrow stone steps led down into the darkness. Where she had no clue, and she definitely didn't care. Especially when she could hear doors opening and closing somewhere behind her. Whoever was looking for her had yet to see that she was there in the darkened corridor.

Calliope slipped into the stairwell and closed the door behind her. She pushed the dagger into her boot. She hitched up her skirt, looping it through the braided belt at her hips to keep it from tangling with her feet. With both hands pressed to the cool stone walls of the stairwell, shuddering at the softness of old and new cobwebs, pretending that spiders didn't exist. She hurried as much as she dared in the dark so that she didn't end up falling down to her death. She refused to die. Not today. Not like this.

She would not be a victim.

At the base of the stairs, she pushed against a door, coming into what was obviously the kitchens with the large hearth at one end and all the cooking accouterments and the scents of last night's supper still lingering in the air.

The kitchen was empty of staff who'd likely fled when the enemy infiltrated the walls, especially now that their Chief was dead. And she couldn't blame them; they weren't skilled fighters, and why should they try?

The Chief was dead.

Except she was the Chief now, wasn't she?

Though she was a stranger, and none of them trusted her. Why should they? In fact, she thought with a heavy, cold dread, what were the odds that the day she arrived, their Chief was murdered. She'd have to be an idiot to think they wouldn't put two and two together and come up with the very wrong answer that she was somehow involved, which she wasn't. Far from it.

Oh, how she wished for her mother. Lady Mary was calm, cool, and level-headed in all things.

Even her escape from Scotland had been carefully

THE LAIRD'S GUARDIAN ANGEL

planned. Not once had she looked scared. Nor really that excited. She'd been unflappable, purposeful.

But no one expected her to die so young, least of all Calliope. The formidable way her mother had lived made it seem like she was invincible, that she'd be alive to one hundred.

There was no time to dwell on it now, no time to fret about the past, what could have been, or what she wished for. Survival was paramount, and she had no one to rely on except herself.

Calliope spotted a door beside a table full of cooking supplies with a darkened window above it. The door had to lead outside. She pushed against the wood, finding that the door didn't budge. Was it blocked from the other side? At first, she feared that someone had purposefully locked her in here with the enemy, only to realize more logically the staff had blocked the enemy from being able to give chase.

Which meant there was no use trying to go through the door, she'd only be wasting her time. Calliope was quick-witted and clever, however, so she pulled a stool over to the working table with the window above it, climbed on top, pushed open the shutters, and peeked through. No one waited on the other side to run her through. So, she put a leg through the open window. Straddling the ledge—how very unladylike of her—she managed to wriggle her way out, falling to the cold ground in a heap and rolling onto something slimy. Oh, for the love of... Undoubtedly, she'd landed on something she didn't want to name. Refuse from the cooking. Garbage.

It smelled of blood and guts and grease. Calliope gagged as she pushed to her feet. She glanced toward where the door was; sure enough, it had been blocked by several barrels. But she didn't have time to look. Running was paramount. Like right now. So, Calliope picked up her feet and did just that until realizing she had no idea where she was or where she was running to, only that it was away from the castle and the evil men chasing her.

In the dark, the area was full of hulking black shadows. Calliope blinked to let her eyes adjust, trying to gain her bearings. It had been daylight when they'd arrived. There'd been a courtyard, many outbuildings, a long stable, and then the keep. To the sides of the keep, pathways led around perhaps here to the back, which is where she suspected she was now —the rear of the castle. But she couldn't recall from memory at all where it led.

If she could get to the stable, she might be able to steal a horse, but getting out of the gates with an enemy lurking seemed not only impossible but dangerous. She'd have to make the journey on foot and pray she wasn't set upon the way.

Instead of running around toward the front of the keep and the gates, she ran in the opposite direction, through the herb and vegetable garden, past a small barn that stank of cows and pigs. She didn't have to run long before she came to a wall made of stone and twice her height. Edging along the expanse of it, she prayed for a gate she could simply open up and run through, but there was no such thing. Why, oh why, did her father have to be so well-versed in fortifications?

None of his careful planning had helped in the end—the opposite, in fact, as she was trapped.

Calliope glanced up at the battlements, half expecting whoever had chased her up the stairs to be pointing downward toward her so far away now. She could barely make out the high walls, and with every movement, she couldn't be sure if it was a man or just visions playing out in her mind.

THE LAIRD'S GUARDIAN ANGEL

There was only one way she was getting out of here: by climbing. Calliope gritted her teeth and thanked her stars she'd actually practiced climbing more times than she could count. An avid climber of trees and walls, this was not where she thought her hobby would lead her, and yet she was grateful for this small rebellion she'd been keen to advance her skills.

Reaching through the bottom of her hem to grab the back of her skirt and pull it through her legs, up toward the apex of her thighs, she tucked it into her belt with the front of her skirts, creating pantaloons. If her mother only saw her now...

Perhaps, in this instance, her mother would eschew propriety and etiquette for survival.

With that thought in mind, Calliope reached up and grabbed hold of the stone, her fingers brushing against the mortar. Next was finding even just the tiniest foothold for her boot. She'd always been sensitive to her little feet, but now, when she needed them to balance on the smallest grooves and anomalies in the stones of the wall, she was grateful.

She hauled herself up, her body shaking from the exertion and the rush of fear and nerves that this evening had brought her. Just as she'd taught herself early on, she drew in a deep, slow breath, trying to calm her racing heart and mind so she could focus on the task at hand.

She'd made it halfway up the wall when the rock she gripped with her right hand came loose.

"No," she groaned low and under her breath as she started to lose purchase with the rest of her limbs, reaching wildly with her right to correct the issue and finally gripping into the hole where the rock had come loose and fallen.

There was no time for falling. Only climbing.

Concentrating so hard that her head was starting to ache,

Calliope continued her ascent until, at last, her hands touched the top of the wall. Using her upper body strength, she pulled herself up to sit on the wall, needing not only to catch her breath but also to see what she was dealing with on the other side, which currently looked like a gaping black hole.

Her heart was pounding, her damp hands shaking, legs trembling. Her breath was erratic, and she was on the verge of hysterical tears.

She had a moment's panic where she wondered if this wall, only twice as tall as a woman, might lead toward a cliff on the other side, which she would rather toss herself into than return to the keep filled with murderers.

She blinked into the dark, trying to make out what was below.

Thankfully, it was not a cliff—but it was a moat. Nay, not a moat, an actual living body of water. A loch, as she'd heard her mother call them. Like the lake that churned near her childhood home in England, only Scottish lochs held monsters.

Her mother had told her stories of Scottish lochs and the fiends that dwelled within the watery depths as if her heart needed more reasons to pound beyond purpose.

Calliope stared down into the dark, watery depths. Climbing she was excellent at. Swimming, not so much. She knew the basics, but she was no expert, and if the current was strong, she'd be swept away.

Then again, being swept away was better than being beat to death at the hands of the vicious men inside her father's castle. As soon as the thought crossed her mind, she could hear them. The shouts, the banging against the kitchen door that had been barred from the outside. They'd be through it in seconds and spot her sitting on top of the wall.

No time to waste. Go!

Calliope swung her legs over the side, crossed herself, drew in a deep breath, and jumped.

The water hit her like ice bricks smashing against her flesh and bones. She almost cried out, except her head was underwater, and to do so meant drowning. She settled for screaming internally as she flailed her arms and legs, pushing herself to the surface.

The pantaloons she'd fashioned out of her skirts came undone, the water soaking into the fabric threatening to drown her. There wasn't time for drowning, just as there wasn't time for falling from her climb. Using every ounce of energy she had left—which wasn't much, she forced her limbs to project her toward the opposite side and the heavenly land.

When her hands touched the sodden grasses on the opposite side, she heaved herself onto the side, sobbing as she did so. She was desperately tired, terrified, and turned around.

In the distance, she could hear the men shouting. But they'd never guess she'd climb the wall. Of that, she was certain.

Being at the back of the castle didn't help her figure out what way to run at all, and given the quickening chill of night, she was in danger of catching her death if she didn't freeze first.

Calliope managed to climb to her feet. She wrung out her skirts and stared up at the starry sky, looking for some sort of sign.

"Which way, mama?" she whispered out of desperation. "Please, help me."

Just then, there were shouts coming from her right. Oh, heavens no. How had they figured her out?

Left it was.

A renewed sense of energy, or perhaps it would be best to call it a will to survive, burst through her, and she ran toward the woods and away from the shouting. Hopefully, she was running toward the Sinclairs.

9

Twilight illuminated the road before them like a mystical path, daring them to move forward. They were only a mile or two from Ramsey castle, less than half an hour at a slow pace before he'd put his knuckles to the door.

"What the devil?" Alistair muttered. Up ahead, in the center of the road, something lay blocking the center.

Well, perhaps not lay...

The crouching figure shifted to stand, and Alistair held up his hand for his men to stop. In the moonlight, he could have sworn the apparition was a woman. The figure spotted them and scurried into the woods—an ambush!

Alistair's gaze darted toward the cover of trees, and he gave the signal to raise their targes, prepared for a hailstorm of arrows or leaping bodies.

"Bloody hell, we're about to be set upon," Duncan groused.

This was the last thing he and his men needed. Had the bloody *Sassenach* and his men really dropped off a daughter to Ramsey or had they set a trap for the Sinclairs? Alistair was not normally so naïve, why had he believed the man sight unseen?

"Mind the road," Alistair ordered as he took off at a gallop toward where the figure had run. As he reached the entrance to the woods, he leaped off his horse, following the figure by foot, shoving branches and brambles out of his way.

Ahead of him, footsteps crunched haphazardly and carelessly through the forest in desperation to be away from him. The figure swayed as it tried to decipher which way to turn, jerking left, right, then barreling straight ahead. Alistair started to doubt this was an ambush. Danger still lurked, for the apparition of a woman must have been running from something or someone. And it wasn't just him.

Generally, in a dangerous situation, the hair on his nape prickled, and his blood filled with battle lust, instincts kicking his body into action, but none of that was happening now. And his instincts were always spot on; right now, he did not detect danger.

"Stop!" he shouted into the woods.

The figure did not stop.

Already exhausted from the battle and the journey, Alistair yanked energy from somewhere within him and rushed forward, gaining on the whizzing creature. The closer he got, the more the shape took form. Hair flew out in long waves behind her—in a fight with the wind—and even in the dull light of the moon, he could make out it was golden in color. A slim, curvy figure.

Was he chasing... a woman?

Ramsey's daughter? Had the Englishman been telling the truth? If so, why on earth was she running away from the castle? Now, the hairs on his arms were prickling. Something wasn't right.

Alistair didn't know the lass's name and cursed himself for

not asking the *Sassenach*, but he thought perhaps if he called out to her, she might stop. Worth a try. "Ramsey's daughter!" His bellow caused a scurry from the night animals who'd been hiding from their stampede.

Shockingly, it worked. The lass jerked to a stop, whirling to look at him for a fraction of a second before she yelped and kept on running.

Bloody hell. He'd done the opposite of what he wanted, and instead of gaining her attention to make her quit running, had frightened her even more.

"I am no foe!" he shouted as he gave chase once more, realizing that was exactly what a foe would say. She was probably smart to run. He'd have told his sisters to do the same thing. Run far and fast, and don't look back.

The way she moved about the woods, it was obvious she had no idea where she was going. In fact, she was making a large circle. Perhaps if he stood in one place, she'd simply dash into him at some point.

"I want to help ye," he encouraged, picking up his pace, the pain in his shoulder screaming him to stop moving his arms.

There were only a dozen paces between them now. Ten, eight, seven...

Without warning, she spun around, moonlight glinting off metal. In her hands, she clutched a dagger and pointed toward him.

"Leave me alone." The words tore from her throat in ragged breaths. Her dialect was English, highborn, and oddly sweet despite how he felt about the English and her clear upset. "Do not come any closer."

She waved the dagger rather haphazardly.

"Careful, lass, ye'll take your eye out." Alistair held up his hands to show he meant her no harm, as he'd said before.

That he wasn't going to lop her head off or ravage her, whatever she thought. He also kept himself from letting her know the tiny dagger in her hands was not likely to stop him or anyone else who wanted to do her harm. The same warning he'd issued to his sister, make it count. Perhaps later, if there was a later, he'd show her where to put the dagger in order to stall her attacker and give her enough time to run.

A gap in the trees allowed moonlight to shine down on her, illuminating her. The gown she had on was soaked, torn, and muddy on the hem. She wore boots, and from quick observation, Alistair noted they were small, like the footprints they'd noted earlier on the road. There were smears on her face, either of blood or mud he couldn't tell.

There was a wild look in her blue eyes, the same blue as Chief Ramsey, Alistair could see. So, this was Ramsey's daughter. Alas, the *Sassenach* had not been lying. That would be a first. And yet, why was she out here running around in the middle of the night rather than safe in her bed?

"I promise no' to harm ye, lass. Ye're safe with me." Alistair took a slow, steady step forward, arms still held up in front of him.

The lass waved the dagger, slicing up the air between them. "I swear, I'll...I'll scream."

Alistair looked around them. They stood in the woods, surrounded by trees and lichen and the scurry of forest animals trying to get out of harm's way. Somewhere back on the road, his men kept a lookout for whoever had been chasing her. From the looks of her dress, it might have been an entire army.

Alistair tried to look casual, shrugging. "Ye can scream if it'll make ye feel better. I doubt anyone would hear ye."

She yelped and jumped a foot back, and he realized that was perhaps not the best thing to say at the moment, for it only made him look like he meant to make her scream. And if she tripped, fell backward, and hurt herself, it would be entirely his fault.

Alistair shook his head. "I didna mean to frighten ye, lass. My sister sometimes finds relief in screaming." He pressed his hands to his chest. "I'm Alistair Sinclair, of Dunbais Castle. I mean ye no harm. I only came to verify that Ramsey's daughter was indeed delivered."

She swallowed, eyeing him up and down as thoroughly as if he were cattle on up for auction. "Delivered?"

"Aye. There was an Englishman on the road with a group of men. We stopped them, and he told us he'd been delivering Ramsey's daughter." There was no point in telling her the rest of the conversation or that he thought the man was an idiot.

Her brow wrinkled, and the pink bow of her lips turned into a frown. "*Sassenach*? But he was here. I mean there, in the castle."

"Aye," Alistair drawled out. Was the woman daft? That was precisely what he said? Why did she appear confused?

"Do you mean to say it was Edgar who murdered my father?"

Alistair did a double take, even going so far as to take a step back as her words hit him as hard as the dagger might have had she been able to sink it into his chest. "Murdered your father?"

Her arms dropped, and she shuddered, drooping down. Every angle of her body exuded grief. "Aye." The word, so small, so filled with sadness, cut Alistair to the bone.

"Ramsey is dead?" he asked for clarification.

A sound escaped her throat, half-gasp, half-whimper as if she'd only just reminded herself of the fact and suffered a shock all over again. Her head came up, her body stiffening. Gone was the sadness and replaced with a violent anger he'd rarely witnessed in his life from a woman. Once from his sister Iliana when she was bested in the training field by a welp she loathed, and once from the healer he'd thought he'd loved when he told her they could never be.

"He killed him," she seethed.

"The man on the road? Did he also kill your mother?"

"What?" She shook her head. "Not Edgar, *Sassenach* did it. My father named his killer."

Alistair was finally catching on to what she was saying. "Your father called him *Sassenach*?"

"Aye, that's what I said, aren't you listening?" She sounded exasperated, and he couldn't blame her. Poor thing had been through so much in so short a time.

Alistair nodded slowly. "*Sassenach* is Gaelic for an English person."

Her mouth formed a little shocked O. "It is not a name?"

"Nay, lass."

"An English person," she whispered. "Oh, my God in heaven, help me." She made the sign of a cross over her chest. "There was more than one, the castle is under attack. And they said..." She shook her head. "I can't say what they said. I don't know you."

"I told ye, I'm Alistair Sinclair." He held out his arm, ready for her to grab hold and shake, unsure if that was customary with English women or not.

She stared at his open palm. "Sinclair, my mother said I could trust the Sinclairs."

"Is your mother...?" He didn't want to rub salt into an open wound, but Alistair needed to understand what was happening.

"Well, she didn't exactly say I could trust them." She groaned. "Just that they were handsome and fearsome." She

THE LAIRD'S GUARDIAN ANGEL

glanced up at him then, as if trying to figure out if what her mother had said was true.

Nothing she was saying made any sense. Alistair briefly considered slapping her to get her attention, but he thought that might not go over very well, especially since he'd promised he meant her no harm. A slap to snap her out of her thoughts would likely be taken as an aggression. And if his sisters knew he was even considering it, they might slap him first. Aye, better to keep his hands to himself in the present moment.

"Lass, snap out of it," he ordered. "Ye're no' making any sense. Tell me what's happened so we can depart these godforsaken woods."

The lass glanced up at him, startled by his demand. But she nodded as if his order had indeed snapped her out of her confusion. "There was an attack on my father's castle. They killed him, and when he lay dying, they confessed to some plans..." Her voice trailed off as if she were reliving that moment again.

"What plans?" he prodded.

She shook her head. "The Ramseys, they need help. Do you have men with you?" She looked over his shoulder. "Only one?"

"Only one?" he muttered, turning to see Broderick standing close. "I told ye to mind the road."

Broderick shrugged. "Duncan's got it, and ye were gone so long we wondered if the wee lass had taken ye down. Couldna let ye get maimed."

"By a wee lass?" Alistair raised a brow.

Broderick chuckled.

The lass in question held up her dagger again, waving it around.

"Och, ye'll take your eye out, lass," Broderick said.

She frowned. "Why do you both keep saying that?"

"Ye'd best put that away," Alistair said softly. "And come with me. We'll help ye."

"They are under attack. I escaped. Oh, the poor people. Bessie and Gregor, we must help them. They've all hidden, I'm sure, as I saw no one when I escaped. We have to get the villains out."

Alistair held out his hand, nodding when she looked at his outstretched palm and then back at his face. "Come along now. We're going to help, but we canna leave ye here in the woods. 'Tis no' safe for a lass to be out here alone."

"I'm not going back there." She shuddered. "The Sassenach will murder me."

Broderick let out a snort, and Alistair shot him a warning glance.

Did she not realize what she was saying? The lass was a Sassenach. But the irony of her fear and statement was lost on her, and Alistair wasn't about to correct her. She was indeed in distress by what she'd seen tonight and, likely having grown up on English soil, had never witnessed any sort of battle since most of the Sassenachs crossed the borders to maim the Scots.

"We'll no' let any harm come to ye. Ye're under our protection now. What is your name?"

She glanced up at him, shuddering as she caught his eyes, and then glancing away. "I'm Chief Ramsey now."

Alistair let that bit of information rest in his mind, for it was likely true. Yet, she still hadn't offered her given name, and if the castle was truly under attack, then they didn't have much time to waste in him trying to coax it out of her.

"We are at your service, Chief Ramsey," he said, playing along with her. There was no confirmation yet if her father was dead or if she'd even made it far enough to be at the castle. They were at least a mile away, and what English woman could travel so far in her state?

Perhaps the man on the road had simply dropped her here, and she'd been running in circles ever since.

"Come now." He stepped closer, holding out his hand once more.

She stared at it and then put her trembling palm against his. He would have carried her, but she might have taken that for an abduction, and she was so skittish he didn't want to frighten her any more than he already had, especially if they were going to get down to the heart of what was happening.

Broderick took up the rear as they went to the road where his men waited. Duncan nodded, raising a brow at the sight of the lass.

"Ramsey's under attack," Alistair said. "I've offered our assistance."

Not one of his men balked, and Alistair was proud of their loyalty and sense of duty.

"Sassenach has killed my father." The lass's statement had every head swiveling toward her.

Alistair was uncertain exactly what he thought of the woman and whether her words were to be trusted, especially in her state. But there was only one way to find out: to take her with them.

10

The giant of a man holding her on his hard, muscled lap claimed to be a Sinclair.

If only she could remember what the Sinclairs looked like. But she'd been six the last time she'd seen them, and this one would have been a lad.

Alistair Sinclair, if that's who he was, had shoulders wide enough she could fit two of herself standing between them. Even from here, with the moon glinting on his dark hair, she wondered at the softness and the contrast it made to the rough stubble lining his masculine, square jaw. There appeared to be a permanent frown on his face. Brows drawn together, eyes squinted, mouth turned down.

Calliope wondered if he'd been frowning so long that he forgot what it was like to smile.

Whether or not he was handsome, she'd not fully made a judgment. It was too dark after all, plus all his frowns, to come to any sort of realistic conclusion on the matter. What she was more concerned about was that her bottom rested on his very hard thighs in a most unladylike manner. Worse still, her skirts were soaked, and she was surely soaking the warrior as well. If he wasn't already annoyed at having to chase her through the woods, being soaked by her muddy gown would be enough to keep the frown frozen on his face longer.

How he'd spoken to her and gestured at her made her think he believed her to be weak. Perhaps even addled. And aye, she certainly felt addled. Who wouldn't if they'd been torn out of the only life they could rightly remember and tossed into a new life that was swiftly cut down? The father she'd hardly known murdered.

Tears stung her eyes, but Calliope blinked them away, not wanting to have to wipe them away and solidify this man's opinion of her.

There was one thing Calliope was not, and that was weak.

But, given she didn't know this alleged Alistair Sinclair who held her on his horse, nor was she familiar with the very land they rode over, she thought it best to keep to herself just how capable and fearless she was. Men were content to believe a woman was dim-witted and feeble; perhaps she could use that to her advantage now. She had yet to decide if she could trust Alistair Sinclair, and she might need to escape him.

Better he continue thinking her addled, and she could have the upper hand.

Besides, she had more important matters to worry over at the present moment, even more pressing than the inappropriateness of her bottom on his thighs. And that was that this warrior was returning her to the keep where she'd just been witness to death.

Except, she hadn't really, had she? She'd only heard what sounded like her father's murder. Then she'd escaped.

What if, when they arrived, they found out that her father was alive? What if it had all been some sort of elaborate joke?

A prank played on the Englishwoman who'd arrived just that evening and been dropped nearly on their doorstep.

But to fake an attack. To fake a death... She shook her head. If that was what had happened, she'd kill her father herself.

"Are ye all right, lass?" Sinclair spoke in her ear in a low whisper, the bristles on his jaw brushing against her as he spoke. Concern edged his tone, but she was working hard not to shiver from the brush of his chin, the breath of air, which made focusing on what he said more difficult. How was so small an act causing her mind to forget how it worked?

Calliope leaned forward, away from his warm chest and his hot breath. "I'm fine."

"But ye're shuddering. Are ye cold?"

Blast it, but he'd noticed. "Aye," Calliope said tightly.

The word was no sooner out of her mouth than she found herself wrapped in a cocoon of warmth as he swathed a blanket over her shoulders and promptly hauled her back against him.

"Often, there is a coldness that comes from terror," he explained as if that were the reason for her shivers. "And I should think doubly so with your wet clothes."

At least Calliope could be grateful for his ignorance of the actual reason, but then she realized what he'd just said. "I'll not remove my gown. I hardly notice it's wet at all." She stiffened, sitting forward again to lean over his horse's neck and as far away from him as she could get.

"I've no' asked ye too, but when we get to the castle and get it all sorted out, ye might well get a change of clothes." He tugged her back again. "And if ye keep leaning over like that, ye're likely to topple right off the damn horse. And trust me when I say my mount willna stop but trample over ye."

She scowled into the darkness but nodded, remaining

THE LAIRD'S GUARDIAN ANGEL

where he pulled her against him. But only because he was exceedingly warm, and now that he'd pointed out her clothes were wet and it was cold out, she was suddenly feeling quite chilled.

Since they were headed back to Ramsey Castle, and her trunks were in her bedchamber, with plenty of clothing to choose from, it would be quite nice to get dry. But in order to get to her bedchamber, she'd have to walk through the great hall to the stairs, and then when she did that, she would see the body of her father on the floor. And before even getting into the castle, they'd have to ensure the enemy was no longer occupying the walls.

Oh, heavens... what if the enemy had already gone and had taken her father's body with them? She shook her head, realizing that was nonsense. Why would they take him?

Why would they leave?

As they drew closer to the keep, Calliope noted that the torches that had been lit on the battlements prior to her arrival were smothered. The entire stone fortress was dark as if to say that the light had been extinguished not only from her father but also from the clan.

"Do ye smell that?" From behind her, Alistair lifted his nose in the air and sniffed.

Calliope mimicked him, drawing in a deep, earthly—and distinct scent of smoke filtering in the air. Where could it be coming from? The castle itself was dark, and there didn't appear to be any smoke coming from there.

"A fire?" one of his men asked.

"Aye, a big one from what I can gather." Alistair's tone sounded dull and even bored. How could he not care about a big fire?

Her immediate thought went to the villagers. If someone was willing to walk into the keep and kill her father, surely they were capable of destroying the village, too. Isn't that what conquerors did? They burned out the villages, pillaged their stores and their livestock, and laid ruin to everything and everyone they could get their greedy hands on.

Calliope peered through the twilight darkness, trying to decipher if she could see anything that might resemble a fire, even a wisp or tendril of smoke. She had yet to learn where the village was. From the road, Edgar, took her straight into the castle's courtyard, and she didn't recall passing any cottages or pastures. When she'd escaped out of the back, she'd barely looked anywhere to puzzle out anything other than the road and how to get away.

"Where's the village?" Alistair asked.

There was silence from all around, and it was only when he nudged her shoulder and prodded her with, "Lass, where?" that she realized he was speaking to her.

"I... I don't know. I don't remember." Her answer was wholly inadequate for him and for her. But that was the truth, and there was nothing she could do to change it.

He grunted with a disappointment she tried hard not to take personally. None of this was her fault. Not even her faulty memory. What six-year-old would know where the village was in a place she had not laid on in fifteen years anyway?

"I've only just arrived, Sinclair," her voice sounded as bitter as she felt.

"Duncan, take two men with ye to find the village, decipher where the fire is coming from. We'll go to the keep."

"We cannot go to the keep," she said. "What if they are still there? You will most certainly be outnumbered."

Again, Alistair grunted, only this time he managed to sound quite arrogant, as if a few measly, murdering Englishmen meant nothing to him.

Calliope wanted to scream. To turn around, wrap her fingers around his neck, and shake until he had some sense brought back to him.

"Broderick, keep her safe," he said.

Before she understood what was happening, Alistair lifted her onto the other warrior's lap and took off with several men in tow.

Alistair and the man he called Duncan parted ways, going in opposite directions. She sat atop the warrior he'd called Broderick, staring after their retreating forms.

"He promised me dry clothes," she muttered, disgruntled.

"Aye, lass, ye'll be getting dry soon enough." Broderick's words were meant to be kind, but she could hear the annoyance in them all the same. He didn't like the fact that he'd been made to stay behind and mind the lunatic lass they'd found in the woods. She could tell. And really, she couldn't blame him; she was somewhat perturbed herself.

Calliope had always been good at interpreting annoyance. She'd grown used to it with her mother and Edgar. It was harder to understand when someone was being kind.

Well, she wasn't one to sit still, and she certainly wasn't going to be the one that disappointed this warrior. Before Broderick knew what she was doing, she shifted and hopped off his mount, landing a little harder on her feet than she anticipated. What warmth she'd gathered from sitting with the two overly heated warriors dissipated, leaving her feeling as though ice had started to settle in her bones.

"Now see here," Broderick growled, "ye'll no' be going anywhere."

She started to walk away, only to have a strong arm lift her back up onto his lap.

"Sinclair's orders."

"I'm not a Sinclair," she declared as if that would make a difference to this man who clearly took his job seriously.

"Doesna matter, lass," he said as if he'd read her mind. "The Chief's ordered us to stay put and I'm to mind ye, but ye'll need to mind me while I'm doing so."

"I'm not a child."

"Then I dare say, dinna act like one."

"What?" She whirled around in the saddle, prepared to give him hell for his insult, only to hear the distinct sounds of shrill whistles.

"They've found something." Broderick's eyes narrowed.

"Shouldn't we go see what it is?" she encouraged.

"Nay."

"Why not?"

"Sinclair's orders."

Calliope rolled her eyes, even as gooseflesh rose on her skin at the sound of the shrill whistles. "What if the whistle was to gain your attention because they are in need of assistance."

"'Tis no'."

"But what if it is?"

"Good God, woman, hush now."

"Those were not Sinclair orders," she goaded him, folding her arms over her chilled chest. She wished she could remove her boots and hose and hold her water-logged toes toward a fire. If not for the fear running through her veins, she might encourage him to build her a fire.

A second shrill whistle.

"Broderick, is it?"

He grunted just like his leader, and Calliope frowned.

"I think we must answer the call, Broderick."

"There was no call," he insisted, stubborn as his Chief.

THE LAIRD'S GUARDIAN ANGEL

"I heard a whistle. Twice."

"Aye."

"Then it was a call."

"Nay."

She gritted her teeth. A whistle was a call; everyone knew that. Why was this warrior being so stubborn?

"What if it is a warning of an advancing army?"

"'Tis no'. That's a different sound."

"Is there no convincing you to see if the village is on fire?"

"I've my orders."

That wasn't really an answer, but she supposed, in his way, it was. Why did Broderick have to be such a stickler? She was scheming up a way to tell him that, hoping to manipulate him into seeing about the people, when one of the men who'd gone off with Duncan rushed down the road toward them.

"They burned out a single cottage, but not all of them."

Calliope's hand came to her mouth. "Was anyone...?"

"Aye, my lady. A few. We canna tell ye who they are. The rest of the village appears empty."

She thought of the maid who rushed into her room and told her to bar the door.

"The clan is very big," she said. "They must have a hiding place."

"Did ye see any foe?" Broderick asked.

"No' a one."

"Could they have taken prisoners?"

The other warrior shrugged. "I dinna know. We'd best tell Alistair what we found."

"Aye, ye take the woman."

And once again, she found herself being transferred into another lap as Broderick rode off in the direction of Alistair and the keep.

Calliope didn't waste any time. She hopped off the warrior's horse and started to run. After all, Sinclair's orders were to stay with Broderick.

11

He heard her before he saw her.

The lass really had no instinct whatsoever to keep herself safe in a foreign land. If he hadn't happened upon her before making the same noise, Alistair might have envisioned a horde of boar stampeding through the night.

But alas, instinct told him it was Ramsey's daughter.

She was barreling down the road, her heavy, wet skirts held in her hands as she ran as though her life depended on it, boots slapping against the dirt. And perhaps to her, it did. She had, after all, borne witness to death this night.

Alistair would give her that concession, though he was damned angry she'd escaped Broderick and defied an order.

Only it wasn't Broderick chasing after her, but Duncan and Alistair growled in frustration as he pushed his horse forward, reaching her just as she was about to run past him. Her eyes darted up to his, determination and fire in their depths like he'd never seen before on a woman.

Without hesitation, he lifted her onto his horse, his mind

trying to reconcile the fiery woman before him as the same slumped woman from before.

"Dinna kick like that, ye're liable to hurt Prannsa," he warned.

"Who is Prannsa?" She stilled as she asked the question, and he took advantage of that moment to further settle her into his lap.

"My horse."

"You've named him?" Strangely, she seemed genuinely shocked to learn that he had.

Alistair frowned. "Do the English no' name their horses?"

"Well, of course, we do," her tone was exasperated as if he were daft when she was the one to have started this line of questioning.

"Then why would ye think I did no' name mine?"

She gave a dainty shrug. The lady returned from the fiery heathen he'd lifted from the road. "Because all Scots are savages." The delicate way she said it, as if she were remarking on the color of the thistles, was not lost on him.

"All of us?"

"Aye." She straightened her shoulders and sat up a little taller as if she'd made up her mind and was prepared to fight him about it. The lass was strange. An hour ago, she'd been a timid wee rabbit, and now, well, he couldn't say what she was.

"Ye do realize ye're half Scots?"

She made a harumphing sound but didn't reply.

"I'm sorry, my laird, she simply got away from me," Duncan said to Alistair while frowning at the Ramsey chit.

"I did run away from him," the lass offered. "Do not blame him for my escape."

"I dinna blame him at all, lass." Alistair left it implied that it was she, he, in fact, blamed.

The lass muttered something under her breath, and Alistair had to hold himself back from demanding to know what it was she'd said. Duncan looked taken aback and was quick to avoid eye contact.

His sisters Matilda and Iliana had certainly tried his patience, and he supposed there'd been moments when their peculiar behavior might have even driven him mad like this lass was currently doing. Iliana, in particular, loved to spar with swords and often goaded his men and the armies of his brothers into fights. They'd had to build her a special training room, and she'd even trained Noah's wife in how to wield a weapon. Perhaps this woman reminded him a little of both of his sisters.

Alistair wracked his brain, trying to recall if he'd ever noticed either of his brothers' wives behaving this way. No memories came to mind. However, he also spent only a short amount of time with Noah and Ian's wives. When he did see them, he was so involved with his brothers he'd not taken the time to notice, other than his two brothers seemed utterly besotted.

Unfortunately, the distance between their holdings was vast. Depending on the weather, at least a fortnight of travel between, if not longer. Traveling there over such a long period of time often required a lengthy stay, and Alistair could rarely find three minutes, let alone three months when he could disappear from his duties on the border.

Upon their father's death, the elderly Earl's three holdings had been split between his sons. The three of them were a set, born on the same night. The fact that they lived was considered a miracle. The fact their mother had lived through the ordeal was beyond a miracle.

Being the youngest of the three bairns born that night, Alistair had been granted the holding in the lowlands. The eldest, Noah, granted the lands and earldom in Caithness, and

Ian granted the lands and earldom in Orkney. Their titles were bestowed by the Scottish King Alexander III before his death, who had considered their father to be his right hand and wished for his sons to continue in his footsteps. Which, of course, they had, with Alistair now serving Robert the Bruce.

"Wait, what are you doing back here?" The Ramsey lass whirled around in the saddle to glare at him, bringing him back to the present and making him all too aware of her body in his arms. "Shouldn't you be rescuing my people?"

Alistair stared straight ahead, forcing himself to forget the softness of her bottom on his lap. Reminding himself that he didn't like to be questioned, especially not by a wee slip of a lass. But considering her situation, Alistair thought he might oblige just this once. Hell, it seemed he was doing that a lot with her. He hoped he wasn't getting soft as he aged.

"I did no' go inside, lass," he said softly. "I merely scouted to find out what I could."

"And what did you find out?" Her tone was impatient, her pink lips pressed into aggravated lines.

What if he kissed her right now? Would they plump out as he'd seen them earlier? Would she kiss him back—or stab him with her tiny dagger. Stab. She'd definitely stab him.

Alistair narrowed his eyes and cleared his throat. Dear God, he needed to stop thinking about her arse and her mouth on his.

The keep. Focus on the Ramsey keep.

The keep's lights had been doused, and the torches had been snuffed out on the wall, but even in the pitch black, he could make out men on the walls and hear the sounds of warriors behind the stone fortress. They were making it look like they'd left, but the castle was still very much occupied.

THE LAIRD'S GUARDIAN ANGEL

"They have laid siege and are lying in wait. Who is your father's closest ally? Who would come to his rescue?"

"I... I do not know." She shook her head, shoulders dropping slightly, hands wringing in her lap.

The poor lass had quite literally been dumped into this upheaval.

"Did ye know your father had only just recently returned from a raid on English lands?"

"I did not." She sounded so forlorn, he almost wished there was a way he could comfort her. "Do you think that Sassenach's castle is the one he raided?"

"Mayhap." Ramsey had been on watch on the border weeks before Alistair, chasing some of the English soldiers back across the border. A few of his men had taken it upon themselves to teach the Sassenachs a lesson, going a little too far.

If it had been Alistair, he would have made certain to keep his men in line. But Ramsey was getting older, and the younger warriors thought they could get away with it. Alistair hadn't been told more than that, but he'd issued Ramsey an order to get his men under control, or it was going to cost him. He hadn't realized it would cost him so soon.

She slumped down against him. "Why is this world so brutal?"

Alistair didn't have an answer for her. No matter what side of the border one was on, there were bound to be dangers. That was a lesson he'd learned over and over again.

Awkwardly, he patted her back, trying to soothe her. "Hush now, we'll keep ye safe."

She leaned against him, and he pretended not to notice her closeness. "Until the next man decides they want a fight."

"Even then, I'll no' let harm come to ye until we've figured this out."

"I have no army. I'm still determining where my father's army is. Do you suppose they've abandoned me?"

That was an odd thing for her to say. Likely, the Ramseys who'd survived were regrouping. Possibly taking a vote on the next Chief. "What do ye need an army for?"

"To take my castle back."

Her castle. The lass had barely been on Scottish soil a day and was already taking ownership. But she wasn't wrong. It was her birthright. Alistair grunted.

"And don't you dare make it out as if I were another English conqueror. I am half Scots, and I am my father's only heir. That castle is more mine than anyone else's."

"If the clan will have ye as their leader. The elders may vote for someone new. I agree, ye have a right to it, but they may no' feel the same given how long ye've been away and the betrayal of your mother."

"Why would they do that? My mother's mistake is not my own."

Mistake. That was an interesting way to put abandoning one's husband and faking her own death and that of his child. But Alistair wasn't one to judge the dead or the decisions they made when alive. What did it matter?

"Because, lass, ye may be Ramsey's only child, but ye know nothing of our ways, nor those of our people. Ye're a stranger here, an outlander. And some may no' feel ye're the best to lead."

The lass scoffed and crossed her arms. "If I were a man, they'd not think that, and you'd not say it."

"Ye're right. If ye were a man, ye'd be dead."

That quieted her, and he hoped he hadn't hurt her feelings. What in the bloody... Why the hell should he care about her feelings?

His sisters must have been making him soft. Now that his brothers had married, he was outnumbered—there were four women in their family as opposed to the three male Sinclair sons.

"Nay, I refuse to believe that," she said, surprising him. "If I were a man, I would have been trained better, and my father wouldn't be dead, and I'd not be here on your horse, Prannsa. You would have never met Edgar on the road and, therefore, would have ridden right by Ramsey lands."

He couldn't argue with her logic. Everything she said was absolutely true.

"Duncan, gather the men. We're going to Dunbais Castle."

"Aye, my laird. They were checking to see if there was anyone in the village after seeing to the croft that was on fire."

Alistair nodded. "Good."

"What?" the Ramsey lass said. "Leaving? You can't take me with you. I forbid it."

"Ye're no' in a place to bargain, lass. We'll go to my castle and sort this out. I will send envoys to your father's allies and your people to figure out where they've gone. For now, they are safest in hiding."

The lass sat forward, jerking her head in denial. "I won't leave them. Let me down."

Alistair held on tight to her. She would be the cause of her own death and the death of his sanity if she didn't quit. "Ye'll die at the same hands that took your father. What good will ye do them if ye're dead?"

She stilled, and the silence dragged on so long that he wasn't certain she was contemplating what he said or if she'd fallen asleep sitting up. Perhaps another scenario was that she was plotting his own demise.

Finally, she said, "Fine. But I want to be a part of the planning."

Alistair almost laughed, except he was very aware of what it cost him when he laughed at his sisters. "Nay," he simply said.

"I insist." She was rather quick to reply.

"I dinna care if ye insist."

"Why are you being so stubborn?"

"Ye're a woman." He rolled his eyes. Why was she so stubborn? "Women do no' make battle plans with men."

"I'm more than a woman, Sinclair, I am Chief Ramsey. You may not accept it, and perhaps my people do not accept it, but 'tis a fact that when my father drew his last breath"—at this, she crossed herself—"God rest his soul—I became their leader until someone takes it away from me."

"And ye would no' consider the attack to be someone taking it away?"

"Not by an Englishman. It can only be taken away if one of the clan votes in a new laird." She sounded rather pleased with herself to have brought up this fact that he had supplied her with not ten minutes before.

Alistair couldn't help but grin. "All right, I'll let ye in the room, and ye canna sit at the table, but ye canna say a word while we're discussing."

The way she stiffened, he could almost see her frown, the pink bow of her lips pinching. He almost turned her around just so he could see if he was right. Who knew it was going to require such a feat of willpower in all matters to be around her?

"I will agree for now, but if I think you're on the wrong path, I will intervene." She nodded as if it were settled.

"Did ye hear what I said, woman?" Alistair couldn't help

the indignation in his voice. "Ye'll no' say a word, or I'll have ye removed from the hall."

She didn't say anything, and Alistair took that as her consent. However, when he thought about it further, he realized that it meant the opposite whenever his sisters were silent.

Heaven help him, the Ramsey lass was going to test his patience.

12

The moment his mount's nostrils crossed into England, Sir Edgar of Bromley breathed not just a sigh of relief but more like a gasp of life.

In fact, he was so bloody happy to have finally made it back to his native country that he leaped off his mount, fell to his knees, and kissed the earth. Scotland and all the heathens who lived there could go rot. England was forever.

He kissed and kissed until a piece of grass fastened to his lips, and he sputtered to let it loose. Meanwhile, his men sat their horses, looking down at him with mixtures of both shame and curiosity. Their leader was quite an odd one.

Well, he didn't care. They were safe because of him.

Another week with the twit and her mother and all their heads would be rotting over some Scottish fire, he was certain of it.

He'd done his duty by king and country and seen to it that plans were put into motion that no one could stop.

Back on his horse, they rode the rest of the way to Bromley Manor, where he'd lived with Lady Mary and her child for nearly two decades. Her death was not a sin he'd

THE LAIRD'S GUARDIAN ANGEL

have to answer to at the gates of heaven. After all, the king was chosen by God, and if he told his subjects to do something, then certainly it was with the Lord's blessing.

And it didn't hurt that he was paid handsomely.

'Twas a fact that Edgar had gone quite broke keeping up with the demands of his lady wife. Only, she had never been his wife in truth, had she? He'd only learned the fact recently, which had helped him carry out his king's orders.

Edgar marched into his house, slumped into a chair, and ordered an ale from his housekeeper.

The great hall looked bleak. Too quiet. Too many shadows.

Even the scent of her lingered as if she'd only just passed through the room.

Guilt riddled him, not only for what he'd had to do to Mary but for what he'd done to Calliope as well. She would hate him, no doubt. Not that he should really care. But a minuscule corner of his brain disliked knowing she would resent him forever. And he deserved it, after all.

He killed her mother. Though he wouldn't say, he was a murderer. Soldiers weren't murderers. They were honorable men who carried out their duties—doling out death—in the name of king and country.

Still, in practically tossing Calliope across the border, he'd alienated her, and likely signed her death warrant. Aye, he'd as good as killed the girl he considered to be a daughter. If the wicked heathens didn't do it, surely the life she'd lead there would. Scotland was a harsh country, and the six years she'd lived there as a child were not likely to have prepared her for real living.

And Edgar wasn't all to blame for this. Ramsey was also not innocent. As soon as his daughter was delivered, she would be married off, putting into motion the next order on the king's edict, in exchange for a handsome sum. In fact, Edgar had passed the man on the road who was to deliver the marriage order himself. No doubt, the vows had already been exchanged, and Ramsey would be counting his wealth. Because how could Ramsey refuse?

When it came down to it, everything was about the coin. Everything. Even loyalty.

Edgar took a long swallow of his ale, staring at the locked coffer that sat center on his mantlepiece. For too long, it had been empty. By this time tomorrow, the envoy would arrive from King Edward's court to take Edgar's report and leave him with a coffer that was so heavy he'd need assistance carrying it around.

He'd not want for coin for a long time. Maybe not ever again.

And he could take a true wife to his bed.

So why did he suddenly feel the urge to toss himself from the ramparts?

13

If the brute thought she was going to be quiet, he had another thing coming.

Calliope had never been one to sit down and keep her mouth shut. Her forthrightness and her habit of pushing the boundaries of every social edict and rule had been a constant trial to her mother.

Just because her mother was gone, her father murdered, and she was in a foreign land at the mercy of one particularly large Scotsman did not mean she was going to change completely who she was.

The war inside her was loud and insistent. And yet, for now, she sat back and was quiet. Calliope would not respond hastily. If she was going to survive, she had to put her impulses aside and plan.

First, she needed to understand the layout of the land and pick out landmarks that would help her return to Ramsey's lands. These roads were wild and untamed, and everything looked the same, especially in the dark. The little light provided by the moon was not enough, and her eyes stung from tears and exhaustion, making it harder to see.

If she were going to return, she'd need to concentrate on the route taken. And yet, that idea was better drummed up than served, however, because every time she thought she'd picked out a good landmark, like a massive bolder, hollowed-out tree or mark in the road, they passed by three more just like it, as if the road itself had been designed to confuse any would-be strangers of the land.

Fed up with not getting anywhere, she finally asked, "How do you navigate these roads? Everything looks exactly the same?" And just as she said, they passed by two trees, both with only three limbs left pointing to the right. For heaven's sake, nature was mocking her.

The man behind her grunted, the rumble of his chest tickling her back. "I just know it, lass."

"You just know it?" She couldn't help the exasperation in her tone. "How? Do you think to yourself, ah, aye, I have passed by the ten identical boulders and three willow trees next to the row of pines?"

He chuckled as if she'd said a joke, which she was happy to remind him she had not.

"Instinct." That was all he said. Instinct as if that were an acceptable answer.

"There has to be more to it than that," she coaxed, short of turning around to throttle him.

"All right," he sighed, sounding annoyed as if she'd asked him to explain something quite difficult. Which, perhaps, it was, now that she thought about it. "'Tis by the stars."

Calliope glanced up, the twinkling lights overhead glowing gold in the darkened sky. Growing up, she'd always been fascinated by the stars, but anytime she tried to ask about them, her mother hushed her, and Edgar said they weren't a ladylike topic. They seemed to make patterns and shapes to her, and they looked different when she was in one place or another. Could there be some truth to that?

"What do the stars tell you?" she asked, at the risk of a rebuke.

"They form a pattern which I follow."

Relief washed through her that he'd not belittled her for her curiosity. As she squinted up, her head fell back to rest against his chest while she considered the star-studded sky. So, she had been right. Perhaps Edgar and her mother hadn't realized, and all of her questions had made them feel small.

"What pattern?" She could make out shapes if she drew one line to the other, but how did one decide what shape to make?

"Well, if ye look there," he pointed somewhere overhead, she couldn't quite make out. "That is the plow, mirroring our work on the land. Ye see it? The handle and the blade?"

Now she did see what he meant, it was fascinating.

"But how do you know the direction?"

"The tip of the blade points toward the north star. I know as long as I'm following that, I'll cross my lands."

Sinclair made it sound so simple. She could practically hear the shrug in his voice.

"The north star," she mused. "Is there a south star?"

The warrior shrugged, jostling her body. "I dinna know. I just go in the opposite direction."

That would be what she did, too. She smiled.

"Fair enough." And exactly the point she was hoping he'd make. The man had just unwittingly taught her what she needed to know to make her escape. If she went in the opposite direction of the north, she'd make it back to Ramsey lands. Except... she'd have to be certain she only left at night. That wasn't acceptable to her. "And one more question."

He let out a heavy sigh as if she were truly taxing him.

Calliope ignored him. "What about when it's daylight?"

"Placement of the sun in the sky. Why are ye asking me all these silly questions?"

She shrugged, annoyed that her actions didn't jostle him, and she prayed he didn't ask her to explain herself. "Merely curious." Calliope stopped asking questions, not wanting to attract more of his curiosity. She'd gotten what she was looking for. When the sun rose on the morrow, she would follow its pattern in the sky to determine how she could use it for direction.

"Dinna be curious anymore."

Calliope could have laughed at his directive, but judging by his tone, he was earnest. How utterly ridiculous.

Well, no matter, she was tired. She'd slept maybe an hour before her castle had been attacked, and the ensuing horror of her father's murder and her escape had left her completely and utterly exhausted. Until now, she'd barely noticed the ache in her muscles and bones. But as they rode, and the heat of the warrior's body sank into hers, she allowed the gentle rocking of his mount to lull her into a sleep.

She was abruptly woken when he released a shrill whistle, which felt like seconds later, tearing her from a dream she couldn't quite remember.

Calliope startled upright, her head bumping against his chin. A muttered curse came from the warrior, which she ignored as she glanced around, trying to ascertain where they were, who he was, and why she was on a horse when she should be in bed.

In seconds, the full brunt of what had happened tunneled back into her, nearly threatening to toss her from the horse.

"Zounds," she muttered under her breath, and even that

THE LAIRD'S GUARDIAN ANGEL

small expletive barely scratched the surface of what she was feeling. What she'd been through. What she'd learned.

She'd yet to confess to Alistair Sinclair what she'd heard the Englishman say to her father. She didn't know if it was true for one thing, but for another, she wasn't sure she could still trust him. Aye, he'd picked her off the road, offered protection, and even went to scout her castle and the village. But, she knew little of the Scots' ways other than what her mother had told her. And if her mother was to be believed, then she couldn't trust anyone outright.

Calliope shuddered, wishing she could pass back into unconsciousness. The constant whirr of her mind and reminders of what she'd been through made it feel as though she was living in a nightmare she had no say in creating. From one terrible event to another, her body and mind had been flung. And now this.

"No need to be scared, lass. We're at my castle, Dunbais."

Calliope blinked, the massive fortress coming into view. There was a strong difference between this one and Ramsey Castle. The keep was nearly twice the size, and the walls thrice. She could have still climbed them, but it would have taken longer, and she preferred to do it with a rope. Fine, she'd get a rope. No walls and no warriors were going to keep her locked up.

"Dinna speak when we arrive," Alistair warned.

Calliope frowned at his odd demand. "What? Why?"

"Trust me, lass, ye'll no' be welcomed if they hear your English accent."

"Oh." That bit of news woke her up a bit more, and she sat up straighter. "But I'm a Ramsey."

"Makes no difference. With the way ye speak they may no' believe the claim, even with my support, and at the verra least they will resent your presence."

"Why would I let you take me inside if your people will resent me? I won't be safe in there. I might as well go back to Ramsey. In fact," she sat up taller, prepared to dismount, even though they were still mid-movement. "I think that would be best. I'll deal with the English on my own."

The warrior caught her hips in his grasp, the warmth of his fingers and the gentleness with which he held her in place a startling contrast to the forcefulness of his words. "Ye'll do no such thing. I've offered ye my protection, and ye must trust me."

"Why should I? I don't know you." But even as she said it, glancing behind her, she realized there was something familiar about the man.

Madness had finally taken over, she decided. She did not know Alistair Sinclair. She wouldn't have known him before leaving Scotland as a girl and certainly hadn't crossed paths with him as she grew up in England. This was merely her exhaustion, sparking her skin to rise on her arms.

"I've offered ye my protection, and ye have my word ye'll be safe. That is enough." There was such strength and confidence in his words that she wanted desperately to believe him. And yet, he still managed to irritate her all the same.

"How dare you tell me what is enough when it comes to my own thoughts and decisions." A woman ought to have the right to speak her mind.

Was it her imagination, or did the man just roll his eyes at her?

She blinked, and he stared down at her, his lips a firm line.

"If ye wish to defy me, by all means, but ye'll only make it harder on us both. I want what is best for ye, lass. I can promise ye protection and that we will lay siege to your castle. I will return it to Scottish hands. I vow it."

Calliope nodded slowly, though she noticed he did not say he'd return Ramsey Castle to her hands. Simply Scottish hands. Alistair Sinclair, the rat, was still not planning to give her back her castle then.

She'd just see about that.

14

The lass sitting on his lap was deadly quiet. Too quiet.

Alistair had been certain it would take an act of God to keep her lips sealed shut, but apparently, she was listening to him. Which didn't actually make him feel at ease. The lass, though she had tried at first to appear meek, was anything but. Though she tried to hide her true nature, there was no hiding the fire in her eyes. There was an underlying strength that, for some reason, she wanted to keep hidden.

The sun was starting to rise as they neared the border of his lands. A swath of orange was on the ridged horizon, dotted with the trees from the forest. Despite the chaos of night and what they would soon face, a certain peace came over him, knowing he'd soon be home.

Every time the lass started to fall asleep, she jerked herself awake, nearly launching herself off the horse. Alistair had to hold tight to her so she didn't fall, settling her back in place against him. He was keenly aware of her soft bottom, which pressed against his thighs, mere inches from his groin. The feminine waist beneath his arm, and the breasts that were just an inch from touching him.

It'd been a while since he'd lain with a woman. And though the Ramsey chit looked like she'd walked through hell and had the smudges to prove it, something about her was all too appealing. Not just the lushness of her body but something deeper and more spiritual.

Alistair shifted back in the saddle, hoping the movement would get him further from her, but it was no use. She only scooted back, seeking his warmth, no doubt. Thankfully, the struggle for relief from her touch was short-lived as his castle came into view.

"Is that your castle?" she asked, her voice soft, tired.

"Aye. Dunbais."

"'Tis massive."

Alistair grinned as he studied the thick walls topped with sentries, the high tower of his keep, where smoke filtered through the chimneys. The place he felt most himself. "Aye."

"Impressive," she said.

"Thank ye." The pride in his voice was thick. He was damned proud. When he'd inherited the keep, it had been large, this fortification central to protecting Scotland's border, but the walls had been weak and the surrounding outbuildings half. Alistair and his clan had built it up to where it was today. A force to be reckoned with, yet still a home to many.

As they crossed over his drawbridge and the people stared in their direction, curious no doubt at who sat on his lap, Lady Ramsey scooted back, an unconscious sign she did, in fact, trust him to keep her safe. Or else, she thought him the lesser of two evils, which, in her circumstances, he would take as a win.

Either way, the press of her arse on the junction of his thighs was a stark reminder of his male prowess, a lusty hunger he normally kept buried. Beneath the smudges of dirt on her face and the bulkiness of her damp and torn gown, Alistair could tell that she was beautiful, lush, and soft. And he couldn't stop thinking about it. A near-constant stream of consciousness surrounding her.

He pushed her forward with a barely disguised grunt and urged his horse toward the courtyard's center, where a groom was waiting to take the reins.

"Thank ye, Prannsa," he murmured to his mount as he practically leaped from his back and gave him a nice stroke on his neck.

Before he had a chance to lift the lass, she swung her leg over the side of Prannsa's flank and dropped to her feet on the ground. Rather more graceful than he would have expected, she showed that she was used to riding and could handle a horse as large as his mighty stallion.

Now, that was impressive. Then again, Lady Ramsey had shown feats of strength that many men wouldn't have. Escaping the enemy, running down the road, wielding a dagger in his direction. The more he got to know the lass, the more he liked her. And that just wouldn't do.

"Follow me," he said.

Alistair turned away from her, expecting her to follow as he made his way through the crowd toward the stairs up into the keep. More than anything, he wanted to sink into his favorite chair before the hearth, guzzle a cold ale, eat a warm meat pie, and nap for the day.

But she was nowhere to be seen when he reached the wide oak double doors, opening one for her. Alistair turned around, expecting maybe she'd gone behind him, but the space was clear. She wasn't on the steps either. Bloody hell.

THE LAIRD'S GUARDIAN ANGEL

"What the devil?" he muttered, whirling around, prepared to bellow her name when he remembered he only knew her clan's name, not her given name. Why had he not asked? Too busy thinking of her arse. Her breasts. Her eyes. Lord, but he was rogue.

Alistair spotted her, still standing beside the horse, his clans' people caging her in, no doubt trying to figure out why their laird, who'd gone away to do his duty on the border, had come home with a bedraggled woman. He couldn't blame them for their curiosity, especially when he'd made it clear for so many years that he had no plans to take a wife.

"Let her be," Alistair ordered as he made his way back through the crowd. He was certain he'd told her to stay with him. Why had she hesitated?

The men and women, children too, who'd been staring at her, backed away, allowing a path for the lass to move forward. She stood regal beside his horse, not even the faintest hint of fear on her features. In fact, she looked almost serene. Her head was held high, her hands folded in front of her. Despite the mud on her face, she looked beautiful. A ravaged vision that would make anyone look twice. The image was powerful. This ragged-looking woman had a straight spine, fire in her eyes, and the ability to appear strikingly beautiful despite all that appeared to have happened to her.

Alistair found his breath halted. His muscles stiffened. No wonder his people had quickly gathered around her. No wonder they seemed as mesmerized as he did.

"She's under my protection," he said, his voice sounding almost strangled as he added, "Mine." The possessive word rolled off his tongue in a way that startled him. In no way had he intended to claim her, and then, at the same time, apparently, he did.

Nods rippled through the crowd at his declaration, and the significance of what he had just said hit a few of them, causing gasps to ripple through the crowd.

Alistair beckoned her, and she walked serenely forward, eyes on him, her head held high when he would have expected any other woman to bow. He instructed her to walk toward the stairs ahead of him. Alistair followed her up, trying to avoid looking at the gentle sway of her hips.

When they reached the top, he held open the door for her, and she nodded once, then she ducked under his arm into the dimly lit castle. The scents of cooking filled him at once, his stomach growling. It'd been weeks since he'd had a warm meal.

They were met inside the great hall by his seneschal and housekeeper, who eyed the lass up and down as though she were an interloper. Alaric sat at the table in the same place he'd been when Alistair left as if he'd been waiting in the chair this entire time. He sipped on something steaming in a mug; no doubt the morning broth Cook made the old man help with his hands.

"The lass is under my protection," Alistair instructed his servants. "Ye're no' to speak to her. If ye have a need to say something, ye can tell it to me. She'll need a bath and to be cleaned up."

The Ramsey chit looked up at him sharply, and he could tell she had a mind to disobey his order for silence, but he narrowed his eyes, willing to wait her out. The glower she gave him could have wilted fresh spring flowers. But it only made Alistair grin. Better for her to be mad than spark the ire of anyone in his clan when they found out she was English. Eventually, they'd find out, but he wanted them to get to know her first.

THE LAIRD'S GUARDIAN ANGEL

They had a hearty hatred for anyone English, given what they went through monthly on the border. There were only two English women they seemed to love and respect, and those were his brothers' wives. Gentle lasses, they were, and quite endearing.

Gentle might have been a word the Ramsey lass wished to portray, but he could fairly feel her vibrating beside him with unspent energy and anger. However, despite the bristle, there was something about her that he was positive his people would come to find endearing.

He leaned down, feeling like she might need a soft word from him. She didn't lean away as his mouth came close to her ear.

"I promise ye, lass. Ye're safe here. Follow my orders, and all will be well."

She was nodding until the last part, and then she snorted.

The housekeeper and seneschal narrowed their eyes, but Alistair only grinned, pretending she had said something amusing, and not as if the woman had just laughed in his face about following his orders.

"Off with ye now," he said to the housekeeper, giving the lass a wee nudge to follow. "Alice will see that ye're cleaned up proper and fitted with a more suitable gown."

"Wh—" she started to speak, but he cut her off with a sharp hiss.

"Later, lass, we shall discuss everything later."

She stomped her foot and marched after Alice, hands fisted at her sides, and he dared to think that if he were to follow her, she'd wallop him on the side of the head.

Once she was out of sight, he nodded to his seneschal. "Give me the updates quickly."

Duncan and Broderick joined him as the seneschal listed

what had happened while they were gone. Mostly, it was the usual things: a few skirmishes amongst the people, a leaky roof. But what disturbed Alistair the most was that there appeared to be someone pilfering sheep.

"Think ye they're reivers, or outlaws?"

"I'm no' certain, my laird. Could be either. But I know it's no' any of our people as we did a search. 'Tis no' coming from within."

There was another, more sinister idea of where the sheep were going—to whoever had raided the Ramsey lands. They'd want to be far enough away from them both not to be noticed, and since they were about to attack the Ramseys, they wouldn't have wanted to alert them by stealing.

"I'll ride out with Duncan and Broderick to the moors and see if we can find a camp or evidence of who it might be."

"Aye, my laird, verra good. And..."

"Aye?"

"The lass, my laird... is she... staying?" The seneschal tried to keep his face placid, but his curiosity made his eyes pinch.

Alistair might have laughed if he wasn't so horrified by the prospect. "She's no' my mistress."

The seneschal breathed out a sigh of relief. Would it have been bad if she was? Alistair almost asked, but his seneschal spoke again, "Shall I prepare a feast then, for ye and your lady wife?"

Alistair choked on the very air he was breathing. "Wife?" he croaked between coughs, and Duncan slapped him on the back while laughing.

"She is no' your wife, laird?"

"Nay," Alistair thundered. "Merely a lass under my protection." He filled the seneschal in on what had transpired on Ramsey's lands. "We'll need reinforcements and will ride out on the morrow. But for now, Duncan, Broderick, let's ride to the sheep pastures to see what we can."

"Aye, my laird."

As they were walking out, Alistair turned around and pointed at the seneschal. "No one is to speak to the lass. My orders."

"Aye, laird. No one will." Given the bizarre order, he gave Alistair the oddest look, totally warranted.

"How long do ye expect that to last?" Duncan asked.

"No' long at all."

"Aye, the lass seems to have her mind set on how she does things," Broderick added. "I only had to deal with her for a few minutes before she tried to escape."

Alistair turned around to stare up at the keep, his gaze searching out the precise window where the lady in question might be. They weren't wrong. And he didn't trust her as far as he could throw her, which, given her slight build, was probably at least a dozen feet. Far enough that she was out of reach if he did.

"'Haps, I should have a guard outside her room," he mused.

"Ye thinking she'll try to escape?"

"'Tis a certainty. Wouldna put it past her to be shooing our housekeeper out of her chamber now in order to shimmy out the window."

And just as he said it, Alistair saw it—a boot sliding out of the window on the fourth floor.

"My God." Was the lass mad? Why was he even asking—he was sure she was.

"She's bloody climbing out the window," Duncan said, awestruck eyes on the keep windows.

"Ramsey, ye put your foot back through that window, or I

swear to all that's holy..." Alistair's bellow echoed through the courtyard, but it seemed to have worked.

The foot went back through and popped a pretty, still dirty, head. Even from the height of the window, he could see her glower. He half expected to see her shaking her fist, too.

And by all that was holy—or rather unholy—he wanted to kiss the hellion, for if she was filled with so much fire already, to put his lips on hers would be like tasting sweet brimstone.

15

"Laird Sinclair wants to see ye." Duncan stood outside the bedchamber that had been assigned to Calliope, not making eye contact.

The man certainly was as oddball as his leader.

"All right. Will you lead the way, Sir Duncan?"

The warrior looked taken aback, his face draining a little of color as if she'd asked him to come into her chamber for an assignation.

"I won't bite, Sir Duncan. But I will get lost."

He grunted and beckoned her to follow, walking entirely too fast down the corridor, rounding the stairs at a pace that was likely to break one or both of their necks.

"Here, my lady," he said, tapping on the door with his knuckles before marching off down the stairs as if he couldn't wait to be out of her presence.

My goodness.

Calliope waited for the call to come from the inside, but there was only silence. She, too, rapped her knuckles against the wood door, but still, there was no call. Rolling her eyes, she pushed open the door and stared into the dimly lit, very large, empty room.

Sinclair's study was sans Sinclair.

Calliope let out an annoyed huff. Commanded her attendance and wasn't even in the room. Annoying. Why bother? The nerve. Well, if he wasn't going to be here when he explicitly beckoned her, then she was going to take this as an opportunity to snoop.

She'd never been allowed in her Edgar's study, and she didn't remember if her real father had one at all.

Not that it mattered. If there was a study, it now belonged to her.

There was a wall lined with shelves, each shelf carrying a book or scroll. The wall with windows held weapons of all sorts. As if Alistair might expect to be set upon inside this room. She imagined him hunched over some sort of correspondence, quill in hand, only to toss the inky feather and leap for a weapon to fill his palm. The sight would actually be both comical and exhilarating.

The hearth was lit, but very low. A few banked logs with glowing embers barely gave off any heat. She shivered at the cold in the room. No blazing fire for the master of this castle. Though, to be fair, when they'd been riding together, it was fairly clear the man was a fire himself. She'd been instantly warmed. And how irritating that he'd kept pushing her away, trying to keep all that heat for himself.

Calliope meandered over to the long trestle table in the study's center, quite intrigued by the setup. A massive map spread out on the surface, and the little carved pieces that looked like part of a game of chess were placed all over. Riders on horseback. Ships. Men with swords. Castles. Mountains. Lochs. The map was like nothing she'd ever seen before. A work of art with leaves painted on every tree and castles carved from wood stood on top, making the map come to life. A miniature of Scotland.

She imagined this room was a gathering place, like a second great hall, rather than the laird's study. Men would come from all around to sit at the table, bang their fists, argue, and do whatever it was that men did. And perhaps they still did, given the impressive map.

Just who exactly was Alistair Sinclair?

What did a man like him need with a map like this?

She whirled as the door behind her opened, and in came the man himself, taking up the space between the frame, his head easily a foot taller than the door itself. Saints, but he was a massive man.

And also, why did they make doorways in castles so short? As a child, she used to think it was so the enemy would come running through and knock themselves out before those within ever had to raise their weapons.

There was a scar in the middle of Alistair's forehead. Was it from hitting his head on the door? Or from battle? She was going to guess the door. There was another ragged scar on his chin, which she suspected was from an actual fight with a person, not a frame, and it was on the tip of her tongue to ask, but he spoke first.

"What the hell were ye thinking?"

Calliope straightened her spine. Her fingers, which had been stroking the horse on the map a moment before, gripped the figure, prepared to throw it at his head. Sinclair summoned her here, which he seemed to have forgotten, and if he was going to command someone to join him in his study, then he'd best remember it. Then she recalled what had happened before she was summoned and realized he was likely asking about her attempt at escape. Fair.

"Excuse me?" She feigned outrage, but really, she had been

about to climb out a window, and if he wasn't going to ask what the hell she was thinking, then she might think he had no feelings at all. Still, a lass had her pride.

"Ye could have killed yourself."

She shrugged. "I've climbed out a fair number of windows and never died before."

"What?"

His shock made her laugh. She would never understand why she liked the bulging of his eyes and the wrinkle of his forehead, but for some reason, it brought her a measure of delight she hadn't felt in a really long time.

"I'd rather not explain myself." She schooled her tone back to boredom, her expression flat, but on the inside, she was begging for him to engage.

There was an awareness of something running through her veins. The need to fight. To run. To reign victorious over something. And if it couldn't be her own castle, then why not this man? Call it exhaustion or madness—who cared as long as she was allowed to let herself run with it.

Alistair grumbled something under his breath.

"Oh, Sinclair, say it louder so I can hear," she pouted.

He grimaced, ignoring her request. "Do ye want your castle back?"

"Of course I do. That is an daft question." Now, she pouted in earnest.

"As daft as ye climbing out the window." He stared at her, daring her to counter that one.

Calliope sniffed. "Fine. I admit to it being a foolish and impulsive decision. But I stand by it. I've yet to fall from a window. I'm an excellent rock climber."

"Ye mean to say ye had no rope?" There was that shocked look again.

Calliope laughed once more. "What good would a rope do

me?" She waved away his sputter. "Besides, that's in the past. Let us get to the heart of the matter. My castle."

Alistair marched toward her, and for the briefest of seconds, she thought he might take her by the shoulders and shake her until her teeth rattled. It wouldn't be the first time that had happened after she'd done something foolish. But instead of manhandling her, he stood beside her and pointed at the map.

"The horses represent our allies. The ships belong to my brother. This is Scotland, of course, and down here, at the border."

Calliope followed the path of his finger along the map. She'd never seen the world laid out so wonderfully. "Did you paint this yourself?"

"Aye."

That surprised her. A talented artist, a warrior, and a leader? Skilled with a sword, but a paintbrush too? Again, she questioned just who in the hell he was.

"You're very talented." Her voice was breathless, and she wished she could pull it back. For some reason, she didn't want him to know how much he impressed her. "What's it for? Keeping watch?"

"Aye. And my brothers and I are aiding the Bruce."

"Robert the Bruce?"

He gave her an odd look. "Is there any other?"

She shrugged. "I've been in England for most of my life. I wouldn't know. Is there?"

"Nay."

The man looked at her like she was addled, but she was telling the truth. It wasn't like her mother and Sir Edgar had kept her apprised of everything that went on in Scotland; why would they?

"Well, 'tis a lovely map. Now, if there's nothing else, I'd

like to discuss your plans for getting my castle back. As you've brought me here, somewhat against my will, I should at least have a say in that, don't you think?

"Nay."

Now it was Calliope's turn to look shocked. "I beg your pardon?"

Sinclair winged a brow at her. "Ye can beg all ye like, lass, but this will be my operation. No' yours."

"I never." The simple words rushed out under her breath. She wanted to tell him what a brute he was. And rude. And maybe he was the one who was addled. But all she could manage to do now with her throat tight with frustration and irritation and fear, was slam the dumb horse back on the table.

Pain seared through her palm, and she cried out, wincing as she flipped her hand over to see a jagged splinter in the center. Nay, not a splinter, a tiny wooden sword.

"My God, woman," Alistair barked out. He tugged a linen square from somewhere on his person and brought it to her hand.

Calliope stared at the faded linen, the embroidery in the corner, and the thistle, which was actually a bow if one looked close enough.

"Where did you get that?" she asked accusingly.

"What?" He glanced up at her with a frown.

The blood was draining quickly from her face and chest. The sting in the center of her palm was forgotten, and she touched the tiny purple bow. "This linen, where did you get it?"

"A gift. Long ago." He was staring at her with the oddest expression. "Why?"

Calliope swallowed. "Who gave it to you?"

He tried to tug the linen back. "Why?"

THE LAIRD'S GUARDIAN ANGEL

Calliope wouldn't let him. "Did you steal it?" she asked.

"Steal it?" Alistair sounded appalled. And his grip was stronger. He yanked the linen square away.

"I made that," she said, pointing and then wincing because doing so made her hand throb.

"How could ye know ye made it?" he asked.

"Because I did." She yanked out the tiny wooden sword and stabbed it toward the thistle. "I sewed that thistle to look like a bow. A small rebellion against my mother."

"Ye..." His eyes widened now as he warded off her tiny wooden sword. "Ye sewed this?"

"Aye. Where did you get it?"

"Who did ye give it to?"

Calliope narrowed her eyes. "'Tis rude to answer a question with a question."

"All right, fine. 'Twas a gift. At a joust."

"By a lass?"

"Aye."

"That was me."

"Ye lie."

Calliope rolled her eyes and then repeated how she'd seen the lad holding the reins of a warrior's horse and that she had been intent on gifting her rebellious linen to a warrior. Still, when she'd seen him, she'd given it to him instead.

"Ye..." he said again as if he couldn't quite grasp the concept that she was herself and that she'd been a little girl once, and not just any young woman, but the one who'd given him a gift.

"Aye, me. Is that so hard to believe?"

He shook his head, a look of awe coming over his face. "I've worn this linen for every battle, every competition."

"Really?" she smiled, intrigued by his admission.

"It has been my good luck token."

"Are you serious?" Why was her heart thudding so hard behind the wall of her chest?

"Every single one."

"And have you won them all?"

"Aye."

"So, what you're saying is, you want to thank me."

Alistair snorted. "I supposed I owe ye my gratitude. Though, I dinna even know your name."

Calliope formed an O with her mouth, surprised she'd yet to share that with him. "Calliope."

He grinned.

"And what you're also wanting to say, Sinclair, is that since I was so kind as to give you my rebellion linen, which has helped you to be victorious and successful, that you wish to let me lead this rebellion against those who have taken my castle."

"No' so much, Calliope."

The way he said her name sent a little thrill up her spine.

"Well, it was worth a try." She grinned. "At least let me... observe."

Alistair shook his head, and she felt those familiar tremors of anger returning.

"After all we've been through, Sinclair, I thought better of you."

"All we've been through?"

"Aye, my blood is woven into that bow on that tiny square. You took me with you for all the other battles."

"If I were no' a sane man, I might actually believe ye." A whistle sounded from the window. "Ah, they come."

"Who comes?" She started toward the window.

"My allies."

Outside, a thunderous sound emanated from the ground. Dozens of warriors were riding toward the castle. She might have been terrified they were about to be set upon if he'd not just declared them allies. "They will help?"

"Aye." Confidence oozed from his voice.

"Please, let me at least speak with them and offer my thanks." Her voice was as sweet as honey.

Alistair looked like he would say no but quickly changed his mind. "All right. But allow me to introduce ye first."

The first of many battles won.

16

On the stone steps in front of the keep, Alistair stood before the neighboring allies, armed to the teeth for battle. His claymore was strapped to his back, daggers in the braces on each of his wrists, tucked into his boots, and a few more through the braided loops of his belt. A targe was strapped to one arm to take the blows of an enemy, and he also had strapped to his belt an axe.

If there was one thing Alistair took seriously in life—it was survival.

The dozens of men before him, too, came similarly outfitted. For most of their lives, they'd been fighting. Trying to keep the lands they'd been born in from being taken by the English enemy.

This was a fate they had accepted from childhood, a promise to both their ancestors and their descendants that Scotland and its people would not be wiped out by the *Sassenachs* who dared claim ownership.

Alistair was not one to beg for help. Not because his own army was formidable enough—which it was—not out of fear —because he wasn't scared. The reason he didn't have to be was because when these men, his allies, called for his help, he answered, and vice versa. Petty squabbles aside, they called a truce when it came to their one common enemy.

"My gratitude for your swift arrival," Alistair called out over the crowd. "The Ramseys have come under attack. Their castle, besieged. They need our help."

Beside him, Calliope cleared her throat and gave him a little jab with her elbow.

Alistair couldn't help but raise his brows as he stared down at her. Gone was the muck that had smeared her face. Her skin was as flawless as he'd imagined. Even her golden hair was brighter now that it had been washed. If she'd been beautiful before, now she was radiant.

And the little chit had no problem whatsoever telling him what to do, questioning his tactics. That was clear by the way she nodded at him as if to say, "Now, remember what I said."

Rather than be annoyed by it, Alistair found it rather... interesting. The first thought that came to mind was charming, but how in the hell would he find a woman who didn't listen, one who dared to tell him what to do, to be charming?

Then again, his youngest sister, Iliana, was very much like Calliope, and he found her to be the most interesting person in their family.

Figured the first woman he felt stirrings around, after the fiasco that was his undoing with the healer, was one that wasn't going to sit idly by and let him rule the day.

Alistair nodded at Calliope and turned back toward the horde of armed men. "This is Lady Calliope Ramsey."

She jabbed her elbow into his ribs again. He knew what she wanted. To be called Chief, The Ramsey. But there was a risk in calling her that to an army of a hundred men, which he'd already explained to her. Three times.

English And female. Two strikes against her, maybe more

if they counted her being English as doubly bad. They might turn around and go home. Alistair couldn't risk that. And she shouldn't either.

"My father," she started to speak, and the entire crowd reared back—including his own people. Calliope's words stilled on her tongue, and she glanced up at him in question.

That wasn't exactly how he'd wanted to inform them of her heritage. Alistair kept his face a mask of nothing, nodding in support at her for all to see.

She winged a brow at him in question.

"Ye're English," he murmured with a shrug.

"Ah, so I have offended them." She licked her lips, smoothed her skirts, and straightened her shoulders. He'd seen his sister Matilda do the exact same thing right before she boxed one of their brothers' ears and even his own. She might have been younger than the three brothers, but she was a wee bossy hen. "My father," Calliope started again. "Was Chief Ramsey. Aye, I'm half English, but I'm half Scots, too."

"Did ye say, was, lass?" This came from The Drummond, an ally of the Sinclair clan, bordering their lands on the north.

Calliope narrowed her eyes. "Was?" she scrunched her nose, then her face smoothed. "Aye. My father was Chieftain of the Ramsey clan, which means—"

"He's dead?" shouted Buchanan, their ally on the western border.

Before Calliope could answer, Alistair cut in. "We have no' yet confirmed his death. Calliope escaped the siege to find help."

She glanced up at him sharply, and hissed, "I heard his murder with my own ears. Don't give them hope."

Alistair nodded grimly, what he heard her really say was: don't give me and impossible hope. "We need them, my lady."

THE LAIRD'S GUARDIAN ANGEL

"What does that mean?"

"They will fight for Ramsey."

"But not me?"

"Ye've yet to gain their trust."

Calliope glanced toward her booted feet, but not before he saw a sadness about her eyes that made him oddly want to comfort her. "That is no fault of my own."

"None at all." There was no way of knowing if the allies would fight for her even if she had grown up in Ramsey's stronghold, but the odds were a hell of a lot better that they'd fight if they thought Ramsey might still be alive.

"Well, lass?" called out Drummond with impatience. "Is he dead or not?"

Alistair wanted to march over to his ally and have a word, telling him to reign in his temper or else. But he opted to glare at him instead, which Drummond ignored.

Calliope shook her head, tears making her eyes shine. The poor thing had been through so much. Alistair wanted to shield her from the prying eyes, the questions, and the truth —the horrible, terrifying truth of what could have happened if she'd not escaped. But despite those tears, her spine straightened, and some of the fire he'd seen on the road flushed her cheeks.

"We were attacked," she said, her voice stronger now. "My father was injured. I... I pray that he has not..." But her words were cut off by a strangled sound in her throat. "I pray that he is alive."

Alistair did put his arm around her shoulders then, and she leaned against him, keeping her eyes on the crowd. "Ye need no' say another word, lass," he murmured. "They will get the vermin out of your castle."

"What if he's not dead?" she whispered. "What if I left him there to die?"

"Ye did the right thing," Alistair said. "Never doubt that. Ye could no' take on an entire army all on your own. Ye need us, and we will fight for ye."

"For me?" Her hopeful eyes studied him.

"For ye, for all the Ramseys. For your father, who was well respected by his neighbors."

Calliope nodded. "Thank you."

"We're allies," Alistair said. "Now and forever." Somehow, tying himself to her that way, as his ally to the south, wasn't enough.

The lass from his youth, who'd gifted him with a token that had been his talisman for over a decade, was standing next to him now. That had to be Fate, didn't it?

For the first time in a long time, he considered breaking his vow of bachelorhood.

※

CALLIOPE STARED AT THE SEA OF HARD-LOOKING MEN. Hard in body, hard in face, hard in mood. She'd be lying if she didn't feel a little terrified looking out at them. These warriors would be her salvation. They were covered in weapons. Walking armories. Did they truly need so much? Perhaps taking one look at them might be enough to make any man run in the opposite direction.

She knew she certainly would.

Alistair's arm around her shoulders was a comfort. And leaning against him when she didn't think she had the strength to stand another minute was a gift. She only prayed that she didn't seem weak for having to do so. There were no weapons on her, save for the dagger she'd stuffed in her boot.

He seemed to understand the men well, and they appeared to respect him. She'd not believed Alistair when he

THE LAIRD'S GUARDIAN ANGEL

said they might not fight for her. She was a Ramsey, after all. But their questions had started before the story could even be shared. Trust from her was not easily won, especially after finding out recently all that she had. The secrets her mother had kept. Edgar's betrayal. The father she'd barely known slaughtered just out of sight. And yet, trust was what she had to give Alistair. Trust was what she had to give these men who claimed to be her allies, too.

Strangers.

And yet, hadn't they established in his study with the beautiful map of Scotland laid out before them, that she and Alistair weren't strangers? That he was the lad she'd admired and gifted with her rebel linen all those years ago. Never one to think much in the way of Fate of signs before, this seemed like a sign to her. As though God, the world, or someone else wanted her to trust Alistair. That he was the man who had come to her rescue when she'd trusted him with her secret as a child had to mean something.

She glanced up at him, the hard angles of his face, the battle scar thick on his chin. A man who'd fought countless times since she'd met him when they were young. A man who had been victorious just as many times considering he was standing there before her.

"We will return soon, my lady," he said. "And when we do, I'll take ye back to your castle myself."

"Wait, nay." She shook her head. This was not how it was supposed to go. "I'm coming with you."

He sighed the heaviest exhale as if she were a child throwing a tantrum, which was completely the opposite of the truth. She was a grown woman, and she'd spoken quite clearly and without emotion—a statement of fact. There was no way in hell she was staying behind.

"Ye canna, lass. Ye must stay where ye're safe."

Like hell... "But it is my castle. And if there is a chance, my father..."

The way Alistair's face changed then, she knew the idea he'd suggested of her father not being dead had only been to quell the men's questions. And she knew that. She'd heard the carnage, heard his life drain away as he spoke. Imagined more than a hundred times the way they'd dropped him there on the floor as if he were nothing more than rubbish. Her father was dead. She didn't need to see that to know it.

"My lady—"

Calliope shook her head and held up her hand for him to stop speaking. She didn't want to hear the truth from his mouth. The horror of knowing it was bad enough. She was all alone in this world, this land that was as foreign to her as she was to them if the shock of her English accent was any indication.

"Please do not say it, Alistair. Knowing is enough."

He nodded grimly.

"I know the truth," she admitted, her gaze on the tips of his boots. "But I still want to come."

"Nay."

"I can help. I'm very good with a bow."

"Absolutely no'. The men will be distracted by your presence, lass, that's the truth of it. They will be worried ye'll be hurt, that they need to protect ye, which will take some of their attention away from the battle."

"What if they do not know I'm there?"

He looked at her as if she'd suddenly started to speak French. "Ye're hard to miss."

Calliope didn't know whether to take that as a compliment or not. "I will remain hidden."

"That's even more dangerous. And given we've had this conversation, I will know, and I also dinna want to be distracted, lass. Allow us to fight, and when we're done, I'll come and fetch ye at once. Ye have my word."

Calliope knew from the stubborn set of his jaw and from the very honest answers he'd given her that Alistair was not going to agree. She nodded in acknowledgment of what he'd said. But, the truth was, she didn't plan for him to know she was there either.

The bow would be her savior, and given she was also quite adept at healing, having trained with the healer at Edgar's castle, mostly out of boredom and fascination, she felt confident that her presence would be helpful. Alistair need not know a thing.

"Ye'll stay where 'tis safe then?" He was staring at her so hard she imagined he was trying to see inside her brain.

Calliope smiled, but not too widely. She didn't want him to realize what he'd just said. He had not asked her if she'd stay put. He'd asked if she'd stay where it was safe. And that was what she planned to do. A safe enough distance so as not to distract his men. A safe enough distance to keep herself from being attacked. A safe enough distance to be a help with her bow. And last, but not least, when it was over, she'd have access to the healing supplies she'd brought with her from England, to tend to the men and their injuries.

"Safe, aye," she said with a sturdy nod.

17

Alistair kept a keen ear for the enemy ahead. He led his warriors through the woods, wanting to surprise the bastards who'd laid siege to Ramsey Castle. An inkling of guilt about leaving the lass behind filtered through his mind, but the sentiment was ridiculous. She'd only distract the men, and likely get herself hurt. Of course, he would try his darndest to keep her safe, but doing so could possibly compromise the mission.

Nay, he was convinced his decision to leave her behind was right. And one day, she'd realize that too. Still, the way she'd watched after him as if she could somehow will him to return with the fire in her eyes... It took everything in him not to kiss her goodbye.

But to do that would shock not only her and him but the rest of the clan as well.

"How many do ye think are still there?" Duncan shifted in his saddle, eyeing their surroundings.

While they had scouts to the north, south, east, and west, every man in the regiment was trained to be on high alert should they pick up on a hint of the enemy that no one else did.

"When I scouted before, there were at least two score." Alistair recalled grimly seeing the English on the Ramsey ramparts. The sight of them, so assured they were in the right place, only made him rageful.

Duncan snorted. "Och, that's nothing."

Alistair snickered. The absolute confidence his men had in their ability made him proud. The day he couldn't go into battle with Duncan and Broderick by his side was going to be a dark day indeed. They'd been fighting alongside each other since they were lads. Mimicking the older warriors on the gaming fields and the fields of battle. "They'll regret ever crossing the border, that's for certain."

The sun was just about to set, and given the late hour, he was confident the enemy would be settling in for bed. Probably only a few scouts on the battlements. The English were never well prepared. Too arrogant for their own good. Alas, that was something he could be grateful for. Let them be as stupid as they liked. Come morning, they'd all be dead.

They came to the edge of the forest, the sky a silver-purple, with few stars yet to appear. While it was dark, they'd not yet be as obscured as Alistair preferred.

"We wait," Alistair ordered.

A few of the castle windows showed dim light from candles or hearths, it was too hard to determine from this vantage point. But it was clear while they were getting ready to settle into their stolen beds that they had not done so yet. Whoever their leader was, Alistair was going to smother him where he slept.

Behind him, Alistair's men were silent. Their horses stood as still as marble statues. The only sound was a slight breeze in the wind. A hoot of an owl.

The crunch of—

Alistair whirled his head around. Who the bloody hell was making that noise? His men, too, looked at each other, wondering who was making the noise, but everyone came up empty.

Damnation. Was the enemy on to them? How? They'd been so careful.

"I'll go," Broderick volunteered.

Alistair shook his head. "Ye take the lead if ye hear my signal. I'm going to take out whoever has come, thinking to ambush us from behind."

Alistair had the best skill at sneaking up on the enemy, so it was natural that such a task would fall to him. No one argued.

Rounding his army, silent as the grave, Alistair searched for the enemy. Any sign of a glint of a weapon. Any sound of crunching leaves, or the bending of a branch. He took aim, but it was a squirrel. He took aim again, but it was a rabbit. He took aim once more, but it was a field mouse.

Every enemy he thought he found turned out to be some sort of woodland creature. Alistair stopped moving. Stopped breathing. Listened. Watched.

The forest was still. Lacking the movement of any humans. Not even the trees gave away an enemy hiding within their branches. If he'd been more of a fanciful man, he might have thought the fairies were after him. Sneaking up on him the way he did, an enemy, ready to slip their magical fingers around his throat and force the life from his body.

But he wasn't fanciful. He was practical. He was deadly.

Alistair was foking warrior.

"Come out and fight like a man," he growled, not wanting to shout to alert his presence, but if he were to be heard, then at least they would present themselves for a fight.

But there was no reply. No sound. Only a gentle breeze tickling the back of his neck, as if Mother Nature were taunting him.

The hair standing on end on the back of his neck told him that he should still be on the lookout for the enemy, and yet, his eyes saw nothing to fight. Alistair scanned the woods, the road, and the trees for a few moments more. But no sound from whoever had crunched against the earth came. Even though he couldn't see. He could feel eyes on him. Alistair counted the seconds, willing whoever it was to reveal themselves. But in the end, it felt like a battle with a ghost, so he returned to the front of his warriors, shaking his head.

"They either hid themselves well, or we heard an animal." Even Alistair didn't believe it when he said it, and yet what else could he do? A few of the castle lights had extinguished. There would be more of the enemy alert than he liked. But each of his men could take on four or five easily. Better to face the enemy they knew than the one who kept himself hidden from view. "We advance now. Sitting here, we're just asking to be ambushed. We need to retain the upper hand."

"Aye, my laird," his men said in unison, pressing their fists to their hearts in a show of solidarity.

Alistair raised his hand in the air and made a fist, and they advanced forward, the hooves of their horses making impressions on the earth without sound.

The English would rue the day they ever stepped foot on Scottish soil, save for they'd be doing that ruing from Hell.

※

CALLIOPE GAZED DOWN AT ALISTAIR FROM HIGH ON HER perch in the trees, where he sat atop his horse. There were several moments when he'd been beneath her that she was sure he would look up. That he would sense her just a couple dozen feet above him. That a drop of the sweat beading on her brow would fall to glance against his cheek.

But while his gaze had roved over the branches, he'd not thought to look higher. Perhaps he didn't realize that anyone would consider climbing higher. It was madness, after all. However, Calliope had never shied from heights. A height was only a challenge she was willing to conquer.

Too bad for him. But good for her.

Climbing trees came as second nature. And she was lucky not to have a fear of heights like some. Still, as a spider, before it leaps, she'd watched and studied. Made not a sound. Didn't even breathe fearful of rustling the leaves with even the slightest breath. She heard his grumble about coming down to fight like a man. Good thing she was not a man, or she might have felt compelled to take him up on his challenge.

Then again, she was no good with a dagger, and shooting someone close range with a bow that you didn't want to kill wasn't very nice. Alas, she had stayed put.

Alistair might not have seen her, but she had a feeling his other senses were keen. The way he'd stayed rooted in place as if he might wait her out, she was certain he knew of her presence. If there'd been even the slightest bit more wind, he might even have smelled her.

What would he do if he saw her? Climb the tree and yank her down? Cut down the tree when she refused to budge? Calliope considered all of her options if he noticed her, and none of them were satisfactory.

But then Alistair had done them both a favor and silently led his horse away, leaving her to watch after him as he made his way toward his men.

A scant minute later, the armies of the Sinclairs and their

THE LAIRD'S GUARDIAN ANGEL

allies were on the move. The moment they were out of sight, she scrambled from her hiding place, keeping her distance as she raced in their direction.

Lucky for her, they'd only been walking their horses rather than galloping, which might have alerted nearly anyone to their presence. That was how she'd been so easily able to keep up with them. That and a bit of running which she also wasn't afraid of. When she was younger, her mother often said with disdain that she'd been a lad in another life. Able to run and hunt and climb like the best of those with ballocks. At the time, she did not even know what ballocks were. Now, she knew and was quite offended. Of course, she was offended back then to have been labeled a lad, too. What was wrong with a girl who loved to run, shoot, and clamber up a tree?

Hadn't her climbing skills gotten her out of the castle and away from certain death?

If her mother was alive now, Calliope would point that out. Her skills had saved her life, and they were about to save the lives of her people, too—maybe even Alistair's men. She paused, her stomach suddenly unsettled, as a wash of grief came over her. If only she'd been able to save her mother, too.

The truth of what happened might never become apparent, but the more Calliope thought about it, and the hasty retreat Sir Edgar demanded of her person, the more she realized that her mother had likely been murdered.

The Scottish army had stopped moving again, startling Calliope back into the present. Not wanting to be caught and sent back, she climbed up yet another tree. From this vantage point, she could see the faint lights coming from a few windows in Ramsey Castle.

Disturbingly, one of those windows happened to be her own, the one she'd climbed out of not twenty-four hours before. Was it light from the hearth, left blazing, and no one knew she was gone yet? Or was it a candle because one of the disgusting men who'd murdered her father was sleeping in her bed? Considering they'd been chasing her through the dark, the latter was more likely the case.

Calliope grimaced. She'd burn the mattress before she slept in the same space as a murderer. Then again, she knew that mattresses were hard to come by, and she was lucky to have one. So perhaps she'd give it to someone less fortunate. Though did she really wish for someone else to sleep on the same space as a murderer? Nay.

Below, Alistair was conferring with two of his men. Duncan and Broderick, she was fairly certain. Hard to say in the dark, but those were the men he'd trusted before. She rather liked both of them, but it would likely be a while before they trusted her since she'd escaped them both twice, disobeying Alistair's orders.

They were moving again, and she had a good idea they were ready to attack or defend themselves from how they'd drawn their swords from their scabbards. She didn't see anyone coming toward them. A sudden rush of fear filled her.

She'd never been in battle before. Never had to defend herself other than in the training Gregor had given her as a child and later with her imagination when she'd snuck off to practice in England. A second's hesitation paused her fingers on the bow. Perhaps Alistair had been right in bidding her remain behind.

However, she'd acknowledge that later because now it was a bit too late for that. With a deep sigh, she forced her mind to quit itself.

Calliope squinted one eye and pretended to take aim with her borrowed bow at the imaginary enemy that could rise from the earth in front of Alistair's army. And quickly

THE LAIRD'S GUARDIAN ANGEL

determined that from here she wouldn't be much help at all.

A swift study of the castle's surroundings proved frustrating. Her father was wise, having felled trees close enough to make a good perch for any archer assassin. That wasn't helpful, however, for her current situation at all. And that was only if they decided to engage in battle outside the walls.

The best thing for her to do might be to scale the castle walls where it didn't appear to have a guard, and then hide in plain sight as she helped with the two dozen arrows she brought with her that she'd found inside the stable at Alistair's castle. She'd thank him for them later, just after he thanked her for helping.

From this distance, there were several places where she could climb up the walls without being seen. The left tower appeared to be the easiest to get to without being spotted by either the English interlopers or Alistair's men if she kept hidden in the trees, and she made use of the shadows on the more, crouching as she ran. But she'd need to hurry. The Sinclair warriors were unwavering in their approach to the front gate.

The battle would begin soon.

Down the tree she went again, the muscles in her thighs and arms starting to ache from the exertion of so many climbs without much rest or food between.

But now was not the time to worry about aches and pains. Sore muscles weren't going to matter if she lost her father's holding and his people suffered. Her people suffered.

Calliope sprinted to the edge of the wood near the left tower, crouched low, and took a moment to catch her breath. The band of Scottish warriors was near the gate. Bracing herself, she darted across the landscape, keeping her eyes on the enemy on the wall and Alistair's army.

Was it a good or bad omen that she was having so much luck today? A part of her was starting to think this wasn't good at all. That too much luck was bound to run dry. And then she'd be in deep trouble.

At the wall, she peered up into the darkness, taking in the rocky surface and the mortar between the stones. So far, the ramparts appeared clear, and she prayed they stayed that way.

With practiced grips and footholds, she climbed the wall as hastily as she dared. There were no shouts of warning, no men who cried out at the sight of a woman scaling the wall. If they did, she'd decided to tell them she was a ghost who planned to haunt them forever, but no one seemed to notice.

At the top, she pulled herself over the battlements, dropping low, only to find herself staring at a pair of boots that weren't hers. Ballocks.

"My lady?"

Calliope slowly raised her eyes to an English soldier. Not a man she recognized. That was a relief because she hated to harm a man she knew. Too stunned at seeing her, he didn't have a weapon drawn.

"Oh, thank goodness," she said, pressing her hand to her heart. "A fellow Englishman. Please do save me from this savage land."

"Of course." He frowned, then leaned over the side of the wall to get a look down. "How did you—"

But before he could finish his sentence, Calliope pushed him hard. "I'm so sorry," she said as he shrieked and fell over the side of the wall, landing with a thud she didn't want to see on the other side.

18

A blood-curdling scream stopped Alistair and his men in their tracks, weapons and shields raised.

"What the hell was that he growled?"

Shadowy figures rushed on the battlements toward where the scream had originated. One of the English had fallen? But how? He scanned his men. All accounted for. The Drummonds and Buchanans were also still within ranks. But Alistair didn't believe in coincidences. There was no way that one of the English had fallen to his death at the precise moment they were about to attack, if not for their presence.

That was when Alistair spotted her climbing over the wall and disappearing into a window.

Either it was a bloody ghost, or so help him, God, Calliope Ramsey was scrambling up the castle wall like something out of a nightmare. A cascade of curses rushed through his mind, so savage even he was offended.

"How the hell did she get up there?" he growled.

"Did I just see what I think I saw?" Duncan sounded as shocked and appalled as Alistair felt.

Broderick hissed an expletive under his breath that

matched the dialogue in Alistair's mind. This was absolute madness.

"A specter," Drummond said.

"The castle is haunted," Buchanan said.

From his mates' reactions, and those of his allies, it was clear that Alistair had not been hallucinating at all, and the damned woman had somehow managed to leave his castle, follow them here, and climb the foking walls.

"Bloody hell," he said. "That was Calliope Ramsey. She's going to get herself killed," he growled again, anger seizing his chest, and something more. Something akin to fear.

"The woman from your holding?" Drummond asked.

"What is she doing here?" Buchanan huffed. "And how did she get here before us?"

"I think the question is, how did she bloody climb up there?" Duncan asked. "Without a foking rope?"

Alistair ground his teeth hard enough that they almost cracked. "That's beside the point." When he got his hands on her...

By now, the English soldiers were peering over the side to whomever it was she'd tossed off and pointing to Alistair and his men as if they'd somehow managed a magical spell that had gripped the soldier, tugging him over the side. No one had seen her. And why should they? Who in their right mind would expect to see a woman climbing the bloody walls?

"They're too stupid to realize we lack the power to kill from here?" Broderick said with a disgusted snort.

"Probably think it was an arrow," Alistair said. "Either that or they think we're all pagans consorting with the devil."

Duncan shrugged. "We might be. This means the wee lady is a murderer."

"'Tis her castle," Alistair said. "I'd have done the same. 'Tis self-defense. Though I wish she bloody hadn't." All of

THE LAIRD'S GUARDIAN ANGEL

their plans were out the proverbial window now. Or rather, tossed off the ramparts like rubbish.

They, too, had planned to climb—with hooks and rope, unlike the lass who was otherworldly in her talent for ascending. They had planned to infiltrate the castle quietly and take them out from the inside. Less death, less damage. Not an option now.

"Think it was her back in the forest that distracted us?" Duncan asked.

"Aye." Alistair scrubbed a hand over his face. The hinges of the iron portcullis squealed as the men inside sought to raise it. How had he not seen her? The woman was not a warrior, a spy, or anything other than a lady, and yet she'd managed to outwit him and get the first kill of battle. Alistair was well and truly baffled. "The Sassenachs will meet us out here soon. Everyone be prepared for battle."

"Should we disappoint them, my laird?" Broderick asked.

Alistair grinned. "Never. I hate to disappoint an enemy."

"And what of the lady?"

"I have a feeling she'll be just fine." Alistair nodded toward the window, where her head had popped out as she took aim with her bow, and started to fire on the men who still stood staring over the side of the battlement at their slain fellow.

Her arrows hit home, and two more bodies fell over the side. The few others there looked up, their shouts of shock and outrage ricocheting off the stone walls.

"Should we go home then?" Broderick jested. "She appears to have everything under control."

Alistair wished he could laugh along with them, but he was bristling with anger, irritation, and, goddammit, worry for the unthinking chit. He didn't know if she was the bravest woman, Hell human, he'd ever met, or if she was as damned addled as he'd thought upon first meeting her.

"I'm still surprised she's English," Duncan added with a low whistle.

"I dinna understand how she got here," Buchanan was still trying to puzzle it out.

"She's using a goddamned bow to take out the enemy, and we haven't even had a chance to swing our swords. I came here for a fight, and yet the lass appears to be beating us to it," Drummond added.

"Our swords will no' thirst tonight. But it's clear the lass has issued an ultimatum. This is her castle. Her plan. We are but the army." Alistair frowned, not liking how things were turning out and yet feeling immensely proud of her for having done it.

A strange combination of conflicting feelings, considering he would have punished one of his men for doing the same, washed through him in a torrent he couldn't parse.

The portcullis raised, the gates opened, and men thudded across the already lowered wooden drawbridge.

Finally. Couldn't let Calliope Ramsey have all the fun.

"Shall we, lads?" Alistair said with a grin as he tossed his claymore into the air and caught it by the leather-wrapped handle.

"A bit of fun to round out the night," Broderick grinned.

"We certainly didna come here to watch her have all the fun," Drummond said.

"How is she doing that?" Buchanan appeared to still be quite unable to work it out in his mind.

Alistair shook his head. "Aye. A bit of fun." He pointed his sword toward the moon and let out a bellow of a battle cry, his men following suit as they pressed their horses into full gallops.

For the briefest of moments, the English soldiers paused, as if suspended in time. Their eyes widened, taking in the sight of the Sinclair, Drummond, and Buchanan warriors, and Alistair couldn't blame them. There was absolutely zero doubt in his mind about the terrifying image they created. They made it so on purpose. Every time.

But the interlopers' feet found footing, their own bellows ripping from their throats as they figured out that advancing was the next step.

Too bad for them.

Alistair never looked back in battle. Never felt sorry for the lives he was destroying. Nor the ones he was taking. That all came afterward. In the midst of it, it was kill or be killed. Maim or be maimed. Surviving meant winning. Losing meant dying.

And Alistair always survived.

The first clash of his Scottish steel against English metal sent sparks into the air. He was well matched, though not evenly, and was quickly onto the next. And the next. In between swings, arrows whizzed past him.

Battling was often like dancing. Not that Alistair spent much time swaying to music, but he'd done it enough to understand that it required a coordinated effort, just like sword fighting. In fact, enough so that he'd had his men learn to dance on purpose, noting that each of them moved more fluidly when they were training afterward.

As the Sinclair warriors moved through the English soldiers, felling one after another, Alistair noticed it wasn't just their swords that took down the enemy. In fact, there were several who dropped after an arrow hit him square in the heart. There wasn't time to look up into the window, to see her there, face serene in concentration, to ascertain if she was the one. And he didn't need to. He knew she was, and though it irritated him that she'd not followed orders, he was also extremely proud.

Calliope Ramsey was mad, to be sure.

And with every second that passed, he grew more and more mad about her.

One of the men took note of Calliope, pointing, shouting, and trying to alert the soldiers on the battlements to the trespasser. But no one seemed to hear him, thank goodness. Alistair charged, not wanting him to succeed in getting the attention of those inside who might attack her. So far, she'd been lucky to keep her presence unknown.

"Ye want a fight?" Alistair bellowed at the man. "Fight me."

The soldier whirled on him, the grin of a madman curling his scarred lips. "With pleasure," he sneered. "Ye look like a better target than the old man."

Alistair replied by raising his sword. There was only one old man this bastard could be referring to—Ramsey. This had to be his killer.

The man was skilled. Damned skilled. Sweat beaded on Alistair's brow. Not a drop before now despite the number of men he'd engaged with. They parried left, right, blocking. The clang of their swords sent sparks of heat to land on Alistair's cheeks. The man's armor creaked as he moved, but despite the ridiculous chain mail on his body, he moved as though it weighed hardly anything.

Alistair was shocked that the English had bred a man nearly equal to him in strength. He ducked a wicked blow, and twisted, swinging his sword. The tip glanced against his opponent's armor, sending another shower of sparks. While he fought this Sassenach, his men took care of the rest.

He wanted to glance toward the window to see if the

THE LAIRD'S GUARDIAN ANGEL

man's bellows had alerted anyone to Calliope's presence, but as quick as the bastard was, Alistair didn't want to risk it.

"Who's the bitch?" the man asked at the same time he tried to kick Alistair in the knee.

That was a move Alistair could have blocked with his eyes closed and legs tied together. A cheap shot he'd mastered when he was a lad barely off the teat. Idiot. Alistair swung his sword one way, but kicked the other, landing his blow on the English soldier's kneecap. That was how it was done.

The man cried out, his knee snapping. As he fell to his knees, he thrust his sword forward, a glancing blow against Alistair's bare thigh. The cut wasn't deep, and luckily, several inches from the sacred blood-filled lifeline he'd watched take too many men away as it drained.

Alistair kicked the killing bastard in the chest, and the man fell backward with the tip of Alistair's sword at his neck. The Englishman smiled up at him.

"Well met."

"Who sent ye?" Alistair demanded.

"Who sent me?" He had the audacity to laugh.

"Neither of us has time for games. Answer the question."

The man licked his lips, which were peeled into a smile. "I have no time for games or answers. You might as well kill me now."

"Why did ye take the castle?"

"Why not?" Even on the ground, he managed a casual shrug.

Alistair grimaced his gaze toward the window, which was now empty. Somewhere in his chest, his heart dislodged itself, pounding against the cage of his ribs. Where was she? Had they gotten to her when he wasn't looking?

"By now, they'll have reached her," the Sassenach said as if he could read the fear in Alistair's mind. "You're too late. They'll kill the bitch, just like I killed her father."

There was a blood-curdling scream as another man's body fell, but this time from the window, landing near the other sentry. Thank the heavens above. Relief washed over Alistair in such a stark release that it was nearly euphoric. She was alive.

"I think ye've underestimated her," he said to the dead man.

And Alistair had, too. Calliope might have spoken with an English accent, but she was just as brutal and willing to fight as the best Scots he knew. She truly was her father's daughter, even if she didn't know it yet. Her father may have only had an influence on the first several years of her life, but it had been enough to make his daughter strong, fearless, and a woman not to be trifled with. Wherever he was, Alistair was certain that Ramsey would be proud.

Before Alistair could stop him, the soldier grabbed Alistair's sword by the blade and thrust it into his own neck. Blood rushed out in a torrent.

There was no chance to get answers now from the *Sassenach*, who seemed to be the leader of this army. And there was no sense in trying to save a dead man. Alistair muttered a curse.

He never saw the soldier behind him coming.

19

Calliope moved fast, fingers nimbly nocking her arrow, raising the bow, sighting her target, and letting her arrow fly. Time stood still as she watched the pheasant feathers on the end of her arrow flutter in the wind. At the same time, an English soldier's sword arced in the air toward Alistair's back.

His eyes widened as he met her gaze and saw her arrow. She could also see from the accusation in his gaze that he believed the intended target of her arrow was meant for him. Calliope shook her head, wanting him to know that wasn't the case. She wouldn't kill the man who'd saved her—the man she'd come to feel something deeper for... But the look of fury on his face was more than she could bear.

"Nay, Alistair," she whispered.

Less than a second later, her arrow hit the attacking soldier in the forehead, but not soon enough. The Englishman's blade cut into Alistair's shoulder even as he fell to his knees, dead.

Alistair's sharp gaze flew to his shoulder. No doubt, expecting to see her arrow sunk into his flesh, but then he looked back at her, surprise on his face as he slumped to his knees. No arrow there. For she would never have betrayed him.

And yet, she hadn't been fast enough. On his knees, Alistair's hand went to the blade and pushed, trying to remove it, but then he slumped all the way forward, an English sword sticking straight from his shoulder toward the darkened heavens.

"No!" she screamed out into the field.

The battle had mostly been over. His men having taken down the last of the enemy, her having shot the one going after him. They'd almost made it.

"Please," she whimpered to God, the fairies, whoever was willing to listen. "Don't take him."

Duncan and Broderick ran, bellowing, toward Alistair, and that was the last thing she saw of the outside as she whirled from the window and charged toward the door she'd barred from intruders. With the bow and quiver strapped to her back, she ripped the dagger from her boot, prepared to stab her way outside if anyone should get in her way. With the fury running through her blood, there wasn't anyone who would be able to keep her back from getting to him.

Calliope's heart was pounding, her breaths hard. She opened her mouth to scream at whoever might be on the other side of the door, but the corridor was eerily still and quiet. Dark.

Not a shadow moved as if the entire castle had been emptied, and only she remained. But she knew that couldn't be true. These men had not come all the way, besieged the castle, killed her father, and fought with the Sinclairs if they intended to simply abandon the holding when trouble showed its face.

THE LAIRD'S GUARDIAN ANGEL

Calliope didn't wait to see if she was alone or if any shadows decided to move. She took the stairs as fast as she could, lifting her skirts out of the way of her flying feet as she descended. Her heel caught the end of a stair just the wrong way, and she started to fall. She slapped her hand against the stone wall, trying to catch herself, dropping the dagger in the process. With a twist, she managed to land on her knee, afraid she would snap her bow in half. A cry of pain rose in her throat as the edge of the stone stair slammed into her kneecap.

My God, that hurt like the devil. But there was no time to waste on pain or falling down the stairs. Thankfully, her bow and quiver remained on her back. She felt along the stairs for her dagger, located it, and continued until she reached the bottom.

The great hall was also empty, furniture displaced as if the battle had first started here. And she knew it had. This was where her father had died, and in the ensuing day or two, the men had not cleaned up.

She drew in a deep breath, trying to rationalize how the last of the English soldiers had somehow vaporized the rest into thin air. But there was no time to contend with that. She shook herself and rushed toward the exit.

The front doors to the keep were heavy, but the pounding of her blood, the need to get outside, gave her an added strength. She tugged as hard as she could, ripping open the door, a whirl of night air rustling the hem of her skirt and flapping her hair into her face.

She shoved it aside so she could see. Knowing that she'd been too lucky on the inside. There would be men here she had to fight through, of that she was certain.

Three English soldiers stood at the portcullis, swords in hand, demanding the Scots who marched across the bridge to halt. Their backs were to her, and no one seemed to have yet noticed her presence.

Beyond the men who'd tried to take what belonged to her, Calliope caught sight of Duncan and Broderick carrying their laird's bleeding body over the drawbridge. Though Alistair was easily the largest man she'd ever seen, they did not appear to be struggling at all to carry him as they rushed forward.

Despite their hurried advance, the intensity of their glowers and barks to move, the Englishmen stood their ground.

That would not bloody well do.

Calliope dropped her dagger and notched three arrows into her bow, trained on the Englishmen, lifted her weapon, and bellowed, "Lower your bloody swords before I end your lives."

The three Englishmen turned, clearly surprised to see her standing there. She trained her eyes on them, willing Duncan and Broderick to make haste, not pause. She would kill these bastards the moment they tried to intervene.

Two looked at her fearfully, as if just now realizing they'd been infiltrated from the inside and that she had been the one to fell at least a dozen of their men. The one in the middle, however, sneered and even laughed at the sight of her.

He would be the first to die.

"Do you actually think to let those fly, little imp? You actually think you might hit something?" He laughed even louder, and Calliope gritted her teeth.

Patience, she told herself. Doing anything hasty might mean missing her mark, and this was not the time to miss.

"Take a look at the arrows in the field," she coldly advised. "And then ask yourself the same question. I do not miss."

Footsteps on the bridge continued. Duncan and Brod-

THE LAIRD'S GUARDIAN ANGEL

erick had decided they cared nothing for the men standing in their way. And she couldn't be happier that they cared nothing for the English threat. They would bring their chief into the castle to treat his wound, whether the English soldiers liked it. Still, she kept her eyes on her targets.

"I'm losing my patience," Calliope warned. And given that I'm a woman, my fingers are getting weak. Perhaps you'd like to test my skills?" Her sarcasm was lost on the men standing before her. The man in the middle simply scoffed, disbelieving that he might be bested by a female.

However, the soldier on the left appeared to have half a brain. He put down his sword, shook his head, stepped out of target range, and knelt. "I do not wish to die today, my lady."

The one in the middle said something to himself under his breath that sounded a lot like "Traitor."

She supposed there was always one who would be stubborn to the end. Not that she had any experience with men on the battlefield, but she recalled the men on the fields of the tournament, and there always seemed to be the one who refused to surrender, the one who came away with the most injuries and was defeated anyway.

Calliope was exhausted. And her fingers really were getting weak now. She'd been training her whole life, but never once had she had to put her skills to use. And today, she'd killed thirteen men, twelve with her arrows and one she pushed off the wall. Thirteen. By God, she would need quite the penance to gain forgiveness for this.

Though it wasn't murder exactly, for how could it be in battle, ending a man's life was still something she needed to pray about and ask forgiveness for. Sins she needed to repent for having caused. This, however, this was saving lives. Defending lives. Saving herself.

"I'm going to count to three," she said, "and then you might as well meet your maker. One. Two—"

"Wait." The man on the right also dropped his sword and dropped to his knees beside the other man who'd surrendered, leaving only the one in the center standing defiant.

Her fingers might be tired, but she couldn't let two arrows fly haphazardly. With a subtle shift, all three arrows were now trained on the man in the center. His eyes widened, perhaps realizing now that she wasn't just a woman with a bow and arrows. But a skilled and trained archer.

"Thr—" She'd just barely got half the word out when he dropped his sword and raised his hands into the air. "On your knees," she ordered.

The man grimaced but did as he was told. Thank goodness. Calliope was tired of the killing and felt drained. More than anything, she wanted to tend to Alistair. Calliope blew out a breath and lowered her arrows.

"Good choice, sir," Calliope said.

Duncan and Broderick bypassed the soldiers rushing toward her, the stairs to the keep. Several Sinclairs came in behind them, snatching the three men who'd surrendered. They'd be questioned, no doubt. Held as bargaining chips in the dungeon. But that wasn't her concern now, anyway. Right now, she needed to—

"Help us, lass," Duncan said, eyes pleading.

Calliope didn't hesitate, she nodded, rushing to open the doors to the keep and beckoning them to follow her into the great hall. She shoved the bowls and mugs off the trestle table, remnants of an English feast. Shoved the knocked over chairs out of the way. Duncan and Broderick carefully laid their laird out on the table.

Alistair's face had gone deathly white. Even his lips were drained of color. The white of his linen shirt was soaked red with blood. He didn't move. Even the rising and falling of his chest was weak. But still, it was moving. He was breathing. Not dead yet. And from that knowledge, she could take hope, even as her heart clenched painfully behind her ribs.

"I'll need linens and boiling water. Whisky. A sewing kit, my herbs."

She instructed them on where to find everything, and when they'd rushed off, she looked down into Alistair's face and said to his closed eyes, "Do not die on me, Chief Sinclair, I won't allow it."

She tugged a dagger from the brace on his arm and started to cut away his shirt, revealing the muscled, bronzed skin of his abdomen and his chest. She peeled away the fabric slowly, gently, not wanting to hurt him more than he already was, until she reached his shoulder. Calliope blanched at the gaping wound in his shoulder, which appeared to be right on top of another injury?

My goodness, but the man had been fighting with his shoulder already stitched up. Was he mad? And how many times had he pulled her onto his lap? Saints, but it had to have pained him each and every time, yet he never winced, moaned, or complained. Alistair's stoicism was almost inhuman.

"Even strong men fall sometimes," she whispered against his ear. "But you will stand up again. 'Tis just a minor wound on your shoulder."

Only it wasn't minor. It was massive. Part of her worried he would lose the arm. The cut was deep, and linens from a previous wound were pressed deep into the tissue. It was going to take her an age to remove them and clean the wound without doing more damage.

With all the supplies assembled, she worked to remove the old wrappings and the old thread from stitches that didn't look to have been there very long. Freshly healed tissue was severed all over again.

Alistair moaned on the table, thrashing, pushing.

"I need you to hold him down," Calliope instructed.

Duncan and Broderick were quick to do her bidding. One at his head, holding down his arms, and the other near his feet. She poured whisky on the wound to clean it, and as he roared his pain, Duncan poured whisky down Alistair's throat to settle him.

"You're no good to anyone like this," she murmured to Alistair. "Be the leader they need. Lay still so I can get you off this table in no time."

Her voice seemed to calm him, and he listened. Either that, or he lost consciousness due to the pain. The latter was probably more likely the answer and a blessing, but she liked to believe she had something to do with his sudden ease.

It took several hours for her to work on the wound, cleaning, sewing, and wrapping. Making sure that it would heal properly and that he didn't bleed out on the table. That he wouldn't have an infection. The man was damned lucky not to have the arm wholly severed off.

"Thank ye, my lady," Duncan said.

"Aye, my lady, we owe ye our allegiance." Broderick nodded.

"I believe there was already an alliance between the Ramseys and the Sinclairs before," Calliope said.

"Aye," the men said in unison.

"Then I shall let it stand."

They narrowed their eyes on her. "Ye shall?" Duncan asked.

Calliope let out a heavy sigh. "Aye. I am Chieftain of the Ramsey clan."

Both men looked taken aback, Broderick even stumbled a step. "What?"

"My father was murdered by one of the men you fought today. Or at least I think it could have been one of them. He was English, there's no doubt about that."

"And then ye came to find us."

"Aye."

Broderick bowed his head and then elbowed Duncan to do the same.

"I suppose we should have known that," Duncan said.

"Lady Ramsey, we are in your debt." Broderick pressed his hand to his heart.

"Nay, it is you and Laird Sinclair," she glanced at Alistair, "your men outside. Your allies. I am grateful to all of you. The castle is once again in the right hands." Though it should have been her father standing here. An ache in her chest threatened to take hold, but she brushed it aside, willing herself to remain strong in front of them.

"Scottish hands," Duncan said with a nod. "Though... ye're pretty English sounding."

Calliope smiled through the tiredness of her eyes. "Aye, I am. But I am my father's daughter."

"And she killed like him, too," Alistair mumbled from the table.

The three of them turned to look at Sinclair to see if he would speak again, but he'd lapsed back into sleep.

"Ye should know, lass," Broderick said, "That our laird doesna let any healers work on him."

Duncan shook his head. "'Tis true. But I think he would have allowed ye to do so."

"Why not?" she asked.

"No' our story to tell, my lady."

Calliope stared at Alistair, wondering what the story was.

157

Why he wouldn't allow a healer to work on him. It also explained the crude stitches she'd removed. They looked to have been done in the field of battle between sword swings rather than by someone skilled with a needle. When he was better, she was going to ask him to explain.

"Now that he's taken care of," Calliope said, "I suppose we should see if there are any more injuries from your men I can tend to."

Despite her exhaustion, she tended to more of the Sinclairs while the able-bodied buried the English soldiers they'd vanquished and worked to reinforce the castle. A messenger was sent to find the Ramsey people who'd fled so Calliope could address them.

While she waited, she rested her head in her hands on the table beside Alistair, and then she fell asleep. When she opened her eyes sometime later, it was to the sound of her name being whispered on Alistair's lips.

The great hall was dimly lit, nighttime having fallen. Before the hearth, his two dozen men were all laid out, wrapped in their plaids. They made no sound as they slept, which she found interesting given that on her journey here, Sir Edgar had snored as if he hoped to wake the dead. In fact, it had been so bad that his men kept nudging him, afraid the noise would attract outlaws who might attack.

Then again, Edgar was no warrior, and she supposed if a warrior snored, he'd alert the enemy to their presence. Was it a skill they mastered early in life, or just luck of the draw?

"Calliope..." Alistair murmured, his head turning from side to side as if trying to find her.

"I'm here," she whispered, bringing a cool compress to his forehead to wipe away a few drops of sweat. His skin was hot, a fever maybe, as his body tried to heal itself. Though he might have a slight fever, his skin did not burn yet in a way that worried her. Still, she poured a bit of a tincture she'd made to stave off fever into his mouth.

After he swallowed, he blinked open his eyes, staring at her. "Ye shot me." His voice was a harsh croak.

Calliope was shocked. Did he not remember that it was a sword that had felled him? "I did not shoot you. I shot the man behind you."

Alistair paused, blinking slowly, then nodded. "He was... His sword."

"Aye. Shh... You need to heal. You'll be well in the morning. Sleep." She tried to soothe him, knowing that whatever was running through his fevered brain wouldn't last.

Alistair shook his head, eyes locking on hers, red even in the dim light.

"They'll come back. I must protect ye." Alistair reached for her, fingers curling around her forearm. Despite his injury, despite his fever, he managed to yank hard enough to pull her down so her breasts crushed to his chest, her face an inch away from his. Lips merely a breath away.

She allowed herself to lay there if only for a moment, to savor the closeness of his body against hers. To allow herself a moment to dream. They were so much alike. And it was Fate that had brought them back together. This man she'd given her favor to. This man who seemed to know her and didn't judge her. This man who seemed entertained by her stubbornness rather than irritated. Calliope could see behind his bluster.

"They can't come back. They are dead. And the survivors in our dungeon." Calliope tried to push away from him, but he held onto her tight. "Now, unhand me."

"I dinna want to let go," he whispered. Despite the fever in his eyes, she was captivated by the intensity of his stare. He was truly a beautiful man.

Alistair slid his hand up her arm, sending goose flesh to rise. She was grateful for the fabric of her sleeve so he wouldn't know how his touch had affected her. Part of her knew she should back away, somehow manage to pull out of his hold, but another part of her didn't want to. That part of her wanted to stay here all day. To see what it would be like if his lips pressed against hers.

"I want to kiss ye." The words were low, barely a whisper dancing over the flesh of her lips, as if he'd read her mind.

As if she'd said her wish aloud.

Calliope didn't move. Kissing Alistair would go against her self-imposed morals as a healer. Healers didn't kiss their patients. But when were patients so handsome? When were they so enticing? When were they the man who had the power to change her future?

Never in her experience. And so, she did nothing. She lay very still over him, her feet practically on tiptoe, hips pressed to the edge of the table. And she waited.

Alistair didn't leave her waiting long. He slid his fingers over the back of her neck, brushing her hair aside in feather-light tickles. Then he nudged gently, closing the distance between them as he pulled her head toward him. Calliope's heart skipped a beat as his lips tenderly brushed hers.

She'd never been kissed before. Never even wanted to until she'd met Alistair. Now, here she was doing the one thing she shouldn't. Kissing a man in a fevered state who likely wouldn't remember. Then again, wasn't that a plus? He wouldn't remember this come morning, so why not enjoy the decadent sensations whirling inside her.

Alistair's lips were firm yet somehow soft at the same time. She leaned into the kiss, her heart beating fast against his chest. Could he feel it? Were the same sparks of pleasure that coursed through her from her lips to her belly doing the same to him? Could a man in a fevered state feel?

"Och, lass, your lips," he groaned against her. "Ye taste like heaven. Ye feel like sin."

Calliope typically might have thought saying such a thing was wicked, that any man of the cloth might punish Alistair for saying such, except she wanted to hear him say it again. Wanted him to tell her more wicked things. My goodness... was a kiss supposed to undo her like this? Supposed to make her rethink everything she knew about the world? About herself?

But just as she was thinking it, Alistair gripped the sides of her face, ending the kiss as he looked deep into her eyes. The fever that had swirled there before seemed to have diminished. Somehow, with her heated body and misty eyes, she felt as if the fever had transferred to her.

"Lady Ramsey, ye take advantage," Alistair said with a wicked grin, then his eyes rolled back, and he promptly passed into unconsciousness once more.

20

"Well, well, our mighty leader has decided to join us." Broderick chuckled from where he sat beside Alistair.

Alistair pushed himself up with his good arm and glared half-heartedly at his laughing mate. "How long have I been asleep? And why am I on a bloody table?"

"Three days and seven hours." This answer came from Duncan, who sauntered over with a mug. "We tried to move ye, but every time ye punched one of us and Lady Ramsey was worried ye'd rip your stitches. Alas, it was the table for ye. Have some ale."

Every bone and muscle in his body ached as Alistair sat up straighter on the wooden table. Where his head had lain was a pillow. At least she'd seen to that, and he was also half-covered with a woven blanket. The comforts of a bed brought to him when he'd been too stubborn in his unconsciousness to accept the haven of a bed.

Alistair took the mug, annoyed that his hands shook slightly in his weakened state. But that didn't stop him from pulling the ale to his lips and greedily drinking as he glanced around the great hall. Where was the lass?

And then he spotted her.

Calliope Ramsey.

She was talking with a servant near the rear of the hall by a door that appeared to lead into the buttery. The smile on her face did something funny to his insides. He was pretty sure she was going to shoot him. Why he thought she was going to shoot him, he had no idea, but seeing her arrow trained on him had nearly split him in two. The emotional pain Alistair had felt when he thought she'd turned on him was nearly the same as he'd felt when he'd found out the healer he'd believed he'd loved before had betrayed him.

Alistair drained his mug of ale to keep himself from admitting his feelings aloud. And then she turned that smile on him, and he nearly spit out his ale as an image of her laying over top of him, kissing her came flooding back. Bloody hell. Had he taken advantage of her in his state?

Was the kiss real, or had it been a dream? The way his memory was flooding, with the taste, scent, and feel of her, he could have sworn it had truly happened.

"Sinclair," she said in that soft voice of hers. The one that belied her skill with a bow and arrow, her willingness to kill to save another. There was a flush to her cheeks that hadn't been there a moment before.

She'd saved his life. When he'd seen her pointing her arrow at him, sure she was going to kill him, he'd thought her escape from Ramsey Castle, her luring him and his men there to fight for her, had all been an elaborate ruse. That he was a fool to have believed it. But really, he was a fool for even letting those thoughts manifest.

Guilt riddled him as he recalled the feel of the feathers

fluttering past him, brushing his cheek, before the tip of the arrow landed in his enemy at the exact moment the enemy's sword came down on Alistair.

He glanced down at his wrapped shoulder and felt the throb of pain where she'd taken care of his wound. An injury on top of another. Bloody hell. Of all the luck.

Well, he supposed he was damned lucky that he was alive. And Calliope hadn't tried to kill him as he'd thought.

"Ramsey," he said, setting down his cup, his eyes drawn to the soft fullness of her red lips. Tasting her sweetness in his memories. Like fruit on a summer day and whisky after dark.

Sweetness and sin all in one.

"Thank ye for saving me," he said.

"We are even," she said. "You saved me, and I returned the favor. Couldn't let my champion go down at the hands of his enemy."

"I am grateful."

She glanced around the great hall, nodding. "So am I. This is not what I ever thought I wanted. To be fair, Scotland, this castle, and my father were never things that crossed my mind. I didn't really know they existed. My father was a shadow figure in my mind. And I've no siblings to ask about him." She cocked her head. "Do you have siblings?"

"Aye. Four."

Her eyes widened. "That's incredible. Are they a lot like you?"

Duncan snorted. "Two of them are identical."

Alistair rolled his eyes. "My brothers and I were born on the same night. I'm the youngest of the three of us."

"By the same mother?" she asked.

"Aye."

Her pink bow lips formed a tiny O. "A miracle."

"Aye, considering she went on to have two more lassies," Alistair said.

"Also born the same night?" Her hand pressed to her middle as if she could feel the birthing pains of his mother, God rest her soul.

"Nay," Alistair chuckled. "Matilda came a few years later, and Iliana a couple after that."

Calliope's sigh was audible, and she came to sit near where Broderick lingered on his chair. "A large family. Are you close?"

"Aye." He missed the hell out of them. With two injuries to his shoulder, he would be out of commission for some time. Perhaps now was the perfect opportunity to visit with the family he'd not seen in many months.

Calliope smiled wistfully. "I always wanted a large family." Then her smile faded. "But my mother never had more children, and the family I dreamed of my father having created when I found out I was coming here was also just a mirage."

"Ye've got us, lass," Broderick said, and Alistair jerked his attention toward his friend.

The idea of Calliope being a part of their family... brought him back to the kiss. How he wished he could have another. How if she were a part of their family, it would mean she was his...wife.

The idea did damage to his insides almost as quickly as he thought it. First, he felt like throwing up the ale he'd just drunk, and second, he wanted to snatch Calliope to him before anyone else could think to do so. Like Broderick, who was staring at her with stars in his eyes. If he weren't as weak as he was, he might call his friend out right now and bring this to a settlement of swords. Then again, perhaps he wasn't so weak after all. Alistair started to rise, feeling slightly dizzy as he did so.

Calliope pushed him back down without a word, turning her attention back to Broderick.

"Why thank you," Calliope pressed her hand to Broderick's shoulder, and a stab of jealousy lanced through Alistair. "That means a lot to me. Especially because we will be neighbors."

Neighbors. Alistair grimaced, not liking the sound of that at all. He wanted to see her every day. Not whenever he needed to speak to the Ramseys as his allies. Neighbors wasn't good enough.

But why did he feel so strongly? It was more than the kiss they'd shared that felt more like a dream. Something about the idea of being apart from Calliope made him want to lay claim to this castle, to her. Perhaps it harkened back to all those years ago when he'd been a lad, staring with dreamy eyes at a lass who was giving him her favor.

But how would the two of them... married... work? Two lairds?

Alistair swallowed, annoyed with the dizziness in his head, which was caused by more than being in a weakened state. She had her world, and he had his.

"Are you unwell, Sinclair? You've lost all color in your face." She rushed forward, her hands on his good shoulder as she pressed him back down on the table, leaning over him and inspecting his wrappings. "All appears to be well. Perhaps you've sat up too long."

Alistair shook his head. "Nay. I need to take a walk. I've lain too long."

"Then one of your men should accompany you to help you in case you lose your footing."

"I injured my shoulder, not my legs, nor my feet. I can walk. And ye can come with me." Even as he said it, Alistair wiggled his toes to ensure he could still feel them, for he wasn't entirely sure he could walk. Both feet, all ten toes, had feeling.

Broderick and Duncan started to protest, but he gave them each a stern look as he swung his legs off the table's edge and stood. At first, he wobbled, and a wave of dizziness took hold of his head. He held onto the edge of the table, pushing away the groping hands of his friends who wanted to help until he could stand on his own. Alistair blinked until the dizziness subsided, ignoring the wary looks from those standing around him.

Weakness consumed his limbs from lack of use from fever. And yet, he was determined to beat his weakness like he did any enemy.

And then he smelled himself. Och, but he smelled horrendous. "I think I should also like a bath," he grumbled.

"I shall have one drawn," Calliope said, not seeming to notice his stench in the least. He'd take that as a positive sign.

"After we walk, if my state is no' too offensive."

Calliope laughed. "You're not nearly as bad off as I was the night we met. Consider it a debt paid after the state you found me in."

Alistair smiled. "Accepted."

They meandered out to the courtyard, one slow shuffling step at a time, Alistair hating every weakened movement. This was not how he wanted to impress the lass. But she didn't seem bothered at all; she was smiling up at him.

"Look at you," she said. "I've never seen such a swift recovery."

"Truly?" He narrowed his eyes.

"Truly." The woman before him appeared transformed. The fire was still there, lurking behind a playful grin. She exuded a new confidence that he'd not witnessed before but that he greatly admired.

"Likely because ye were treating the English," Alistair teased.

She tapped her chin in mock contemplation. "Perhaps that is the case."

With every step, Alistair felt his body renewing itself. Perhaps it was the fresh air, but he liked to think her company was making him feel more whole. "Do ye plan to stay, lass?"

"Here at Ramsey?" She nodded before he could confirm. "This is my home. The only home I have. And while you were getting your beauty rest—"

"Hey now," he laughed.

Calliope chuckled, "My people returned. Bessie and Gregor, thank goodness. We buried those lost in the fire and started to rebuild what the evil men destroyed."

A sense of pride filled Alistair's chest. Just as she'd won him and his men over, she'd also won over her father's people. Her people. Still, he wondered if that would be enough for her. She'd left behind a world she'd grown accustomed to. "What of your home in England?"

"Sir Edgar made it clear I wasn't to return. And to be honest, I fear Edgar may have had something to do with my mother's death." She bit her lip, and he could tell there was more she wanted to tell him, but that something was holding her back. Was it something to do with what she'd overheard the *Sassenach* confess to when he'd killed her father?

"I had planned to tell my father about it, to allow him to decide what to do, but then, well, you know what happened."

"What will ye do?"

"I will write to Edgar's liege. Edgar is but as a landed knight and under the loyalty of the Earl of Hardwyck. Though, I'm not certain it will help, as I believe he was following orders. There is not much I can do. Nor really

THE LAIRD'S GUARDIAN ANGEL

anything I believe they will do to investigate. It is all heresy on my part, and if it was by order, then I have no standing to argue."

Alistair nodded. "I canna imagine they would order your mother's death."

Calliope shook her head. "I cannot either. I wonder if there was perhaps a misunderstanding." There was a sadness in her voice, and Alistair wanted to rage against her stepsire. Wished he hadn't let him go when he'd had the chance.

"I fought with the man who killed your father," he said. "He admitted it to me. I ended his life."

Calliope nodded. "Thank you."

"I am sorry, lass."

"I know, but it was not your fault. The *Sassenachs* had a plan. They had their orders from the king. My father was to be paid money, and I think that man was to be my husband by order of King Edward. I think he was killed for refusing. Not something I can say for Sir Edgar, who appeared more willing to take the coin."

"Sir Edgar will get what is coming to him."

"I pray he pays a penance."

Alistair took her hand in his out of instinct, rubbing his thumb over her knuckles. She didn't pull away and, in fact, held him tighter.

"So far here, the servants have returned, and the people have come out of hiding to work the land again and tend the cows and sheep. Ramsey lands are healing. And I, too, will heal."

"Will they entrust their loyalty to ye?"

"They already have while you slept." She smiled. "It was such an honor. There was only one thing they said that made me weary."

"What?" Alistair would do whatever he could to make them trust in her.

"They want me to marry a Ramsey to solidify my placement." She frowned, and on that admission, she did tug her hand away. "But doing that would mean possibly giving that man leadership."

Alistair felt the acuteness of the loss of her hold and wanted them to stop in their tracks so he could take both her hands in his and tug her closer. To admit what his heart was pounding out in a staccato beat. But he managed to control himself with a murmured, "'Twould."

"I want to lead."

"No' many believe a woman should. Though ye've proven yourself more than capable, lass."

"I agree. Especially with the acts I had to commit during the siege." She crossed herself. "I know killing is necessary, but I just never thought it would be so hard."

Alistair did stop now, turning to face her. "'Tis never easy, lass. Even for me. In the dark moments of battle, we must set aside our feelings, but after, we are haunted by what we've done."

"How do you heal from it?"

"Time. And by looking around me. By seeing my people are safe. That is the treasure, really, the prize for being victorious. Life."

Calliope nodded. "And they are living. Most of them."

Alistair took her hand once more and tugged her toward the gate. He needed the walls that surrounded them to disappear so he could feel as though he could breathe, as if the land outside, the open space, would make him heal faster.

They stepped through the castle gate, their footfalls tapping against the drawbridge's wood. He paused in the center, gripping the handrail and drawing in a heavy breath.

THE LAIRD'S GUARDIAN ANGEL

"Are you all right?" she asked.

"I'm sorry, lass, that ye had to do those things. That ye were put in that position."

Calliope leaned her hip against the rail, looking off into the distance. She studied their surroundings as if trying to memorize or recall every oak and blade of grass.

"None of this was your fault," she said. "If anything, what happened to you is my fault. You wouldn't have been injured if I'd not asked you for help."

"If ye'd no' asked for my help, there's no telling what might have happened."

She nodded. "I'd be dead, most likely. I escaped, but they were sure to be on my heels. And if I'd returned alone, as skilled as I am with a bow, I'd not have been able to fight them all."

"Where did ye learn to fight like that?" Alistair sucked in a heady cold breath.

"Here, I meant to give you this inside." She held out a small linen-wrapped parcel.

Alistair took the offering, opening it up to find a slice of honeycomb.

"Honey has healing properties," she said. "And it will give you a little energy."

He smiled. It'd been ages since he'd had honeycomb. The last time had been with his sisters. They'd been staying with him as he and his brothers rotated their raising, and on a ride, they'd seen a massive beehive. He'd climbed a tree with a smoking branch in hand, waiting for the bees to leave so he could reach inside the hive to retrieve the honey, and then they'd ridden like hell, each of them drunk on honey by the time they got back to the castle.

Alistair popped the honeycomb into his mouth, chewing on the wax, the sweetness dripping over his tongue.

"Thank ye," he said. "I already feel better." He wasn't sure whether or not that was simply by being in her presence.

"Good. You look a lot better, too. Though, to be fair, you were lying unconscious on a table."

"No' the whole time." He eyed her, wondering if his memory had been but a dream. But the way her cheeks flamed red was enough of an answer to know that, no, indeed, they had kissed.

And it had been glorious. Alistair had kissed a fair number of women in the course of his life. But none held even a candle to Calliope's passion.

"I'm sorry for taking advantage of you," she said, though the curve of her lip was almost mischievous. Was she genuinely sorry? He didn't think so.

"I'm not. In fact," Alistair slid closer, grateful for the sturdiness of the wooden rail as being around her seemed to make his dizziness return. "I wish I'd been more conscious when it happened."

She snorted a laugh, her golden head falling back to expose the column of her soft throat. A throat he wanted to run his tongue over. "You're teasing me. I should have known better than to kiss a man in a fever."

"Perhaps that kiss brought me out of the fever." He wiggled his brows, somewhat teasing, but his gaze fell to stare at her lips with an intensity that made his blood rush through his veins. Saints, but he wanted to kiss her again. Desperately. To claim her mouth once and for all. To tell the Ramseys she wasn't marrying one of them but him. That she was his forever.

"Ah, so you're saying I have magical healing properties," she teased, though it was said softly, a hint of desire in the syllables.

"Or perhaps your kiss does," he murmured, scooting even

closer, his fingers sliding over hers where they rested on the railing. "Shall we try again to see if one more kiss makes my injury disappear?"

Calliope shook her head. "That is impossible." But when she said it, her eyes were on his lips, and though her words were not favorable, everything about how she leaned closer was.

A fire lit inside him. "Only one way to find out, Calliope."

Calliope glanced up at him, eyes cloudy with desire. "Sinclair..." She'd used his name before, yet now seemed to be reminding herself with the formality of his position that they should remain distant. But her body language said the very opposite as she licked her lips.

"Alistair, sweetheart. Our lips have touched. I think ye've earned the right to call me by name."

Calliope seemed to struggle with this. Trying to decide if she should give in or bolster on with the distancing. But then, she whispered, "Alistair..."

He closed the distance between them, their hips touching where they leaned against the rail, and a spark of hot desire coursed through him.

"I want to kiss ye again, Calliope," he whispered, his face bending slightly closer. "Do ye want to kiss me?"

Calliope's fingers caressed her lip as she stared up at him, passion filling her eyes as her gaze slid from his to his lips and back.

Alistair didn't know if it was the memory of her kiss or the desire burning in her gaze that was his undoing. And he was still determining if it mattered. Everything about this woman reached out and grabbed hold of him. As if he were captive to her very being and soul.

"Aye," she whispered, and he felt as though his insides snapped.

Alistair slid his fingers along her neck, pushing the softness of her hair away from her skin, feeling the hitch in her pulse just beneath her flesh. She stepped forward, with the tips of her boots pushing into his as he descended. My God, he didn't even know how much he'd wanted this kiss until now.

Brushing his lips over hers, a fire ignited between them, consuming him. Burning him. Branding him. He rested his mouth on Calliope's, sucking in a breath through his nose as if she were the breath of air he'd been needing after leaving the castle. As if the walls falling away weren't the thing that would save him but her kiss.

Calliope sighed heavily, her fingers pressing to his arms, curling against his bicep. Passion grew between them, practically crackling the air with sparks as if they two were a flame about to combust.

If he wasn't careful, he might melt along with her.

Alistair deepened the kiss, sliding his tongue over her plump lips, teasing the crease of her mouth to open for him. He gripped tight to her waist, wanting to crush her to him, to feel the length of her body against his. To never let her go.

He was aware, somewhere in the back of his mind, that they were out in the open. Just through the gate behind them on the bridge were his men and her clan. Anyone on the battlements might witness what was happening between them.

And yet, he couldn't find the strength to stop.

Then, a sweet, soft moan from the back of her throat rumbled against him, and he nearly lost his mind. Alistair let out a low growl, wanting her to know he liked this kiss just as much as she did.

Alistair licked at her lips, probing, pressing, asking. And she answered, opening her mouth, her tongue darting out boldly to tease his in the exact same move. The lass was made for him. Bold. She was as willing to notch her bow and let her arrow fly as she was to show her passion in a kiss as deep and intoxicating as this.

Their tongues stroked, teased, tracing, learning every part of each other's mouth. Calliope tasted sweet like the honey he'd consumed, and he wondered if she'd snuck a bite before offering it to him. He could kiss this woman every day for the rest of his life. A thought that before now he might have found terrifying, but now found to be a gift sent from the heavens.

Calliope's hands moved from his arms to his chest, massaging as she traced the outline of his muscles, squeezing as if trying to decipher the differences in their bodies. Her curiosity was delicious and intoxicating. He tensed, enjoying every second, never having reacted to a woman's touch the way he did with Calliope.

He wanted her. Desire pulsed deep inside him, rushing to his groin. At the slightest provocation, he might make love to her on the bridge right here and now. Knowing that if he pressed his hard shaft against her, all bets were off, he tried to keep his body stiff, away from her, but every second of her tongue on his, her roving hands made it harder and harder to keep himself under control.

"Calliope," he murmured against her lips, loving the feel and taste of this warrior woman. The confession tumbled from his lips. "I want ye."

She pulled away, looking up at him, dazed. "What does that mean?"

Och, how he would have loved to explain it to her... but she'd likely run screaming or maybe faint. Then again, Calliope was not the type of woman to faint. She was the type of woman to fight.

"Ye canna kill me," he answered.

She laughed. "That is the last thing on my mind."

"Good."

"Does wanting me have to do with kissing?"

"Aye."

She nodded, her cheeks flaming red. "Then I think I understand. And I want you too."

21

After her admission, Calliope got cold feet.

A rush of nerves seized her body, and she backed away. "I'll get Duncan for you," she muttered before turning around in a cloud of cowardice and rushing toward the gate.

"Calliope, wait," Alistair called after her, confusion laced in his voice. But she couldn't worry about his confusion when she had her own filtering through her.

Why was she running? Why was she suddenly scared? No one, not even Bryce back in England, whom she was supposed to marry, made her feel the way Alistair did. His kiss was... magic. And the way he smiled at her made her entire body tingle with anticipation.

Yet, the moment she confessed to wanting him had been when she'd panicked. What if he only wanted her for kissing? What if the feelings swirling around in her mind weren't reciprocated? Being as naïve as she was in the ways of love, there was a good chance she was completely mistaken in his intent.

Fortunately, Duncan and Broderick didn't seem to have

listened when Alistair told them to remain inside, and they hovered around the gate.

"My lady?" Broderick stepped forward, concern etched in the corners of his eyes.

Calliope smiled at him, hoping to ease whatever worry he might have had. "Your laird will need assistance. There's a chamber on the level above the great hall that I had Bessie prepare for him. If you could see, he is brought there to rest." She didn't wait to see them collect him.

She hurried into the castle courtyard, keeping her mind occupied with other things and forcing her thoughts of Alistair out. There was much to do with the setting up of the castle, returning it to its rights, and holding a vigil for her father. No one knew what the English who'd laid siege to the castle had done with his body. A search yielded no results, so they held a service over an empty grave.

There were tears from many, including her. She was not mourning the man she knew but the man she'd never know.

Whatever memories her mother had given her, Calliope had no reason to believe them to be true. And she'd been so young the last time she was in Scotland that she couldn't be sure if the fleeting images of her father that played behind her eyes were real or imagined.

What she did know was that he was beloved by his people and that he had allies like the Sinclairs, Drummonds, and Buchanans. That must have meant he was important to them and well-respected in the world. It also meant that she, too, had allies.

The outpouring of support she received from the people was heartwarming, encouraging, and totally unexpected. At night, she'd lain awake thinking they would call her an interloper, an outsider. That they'd tell her one of their own should lead the clan.

And to be fair, she was starting to think the latter might have been best.

But then came the suggestion that instead of someone else ruling her stead, she get married. And though all of the potential grooms they'd thrust before her had been nice, pleasant to look at even, none had held a candle to Alistair.

Perhaps that was the other reason why she'd run. She may have wanted Alistair for her own, but she couldn't have him. Could she?

The elders of the clan had been very specific about her marrying a Ramsey.

Calliope slipped into the castle, nodding to the staff as they called out to her, but rushed up to her bedchamber. She needed a moment to think. To figure out exactly what it was that she wanted.

At no moment in her life had she ever been in charge of her own Fate. And quite honestly, she wasn't sure if she was right now either.

When her mother took her away from Scotland, that was not her decision. Marrying Bryce had not been her choice either. The purpose of her journey to Scotland had not been her own. Her stepsire had wanted to be rid of her, and in her mourning over her mother, she'd not had a say. To be fair, she wouldn't have had a say besides. Women never did.

And when she'd arrived, she'd wanted to get to know her father, the people in the clan she'd been gone from for so long. Only that, too, had been ripped from her.

Thrust into a position of power she wasn't certain she'd wanted. As they'd learned about how she'd felled the enemy, the respect of her had grown. But was it what she wanted?

There had been a thousand small rebellions that she'd made in her life. Learning to climb. Mastering a bow and arrow. Sewing her symbol into the linen square she'd gifted a lad.

Calliope couldn't help but think that meant something. When all of her rebellions were added up, they led her to one man: Alistair Sinclair.

A pillar in her life, not just the last sennight since she'd first escaped the siege. But a lad she'd thought of often when she was growing up. The first one she'd given her favor to. She'd wondered if he'd ever noticed the symbol. If he'd kept the embroidered linen.

And he had. In fact, he claimed it had never left him for every battle. That her gift was a talisman to him.

Why was she ignoring all the signs and trying to push aside her feelings? Calliope walked swiftly to the window in her bedchamber, which had the perfect view of the courtyard and the gate. Duncan and Broderick stood with Alistair, who was clearly refusing to be put to bed. And that made her smile. The man was just as stubborn as she was.

Calliope had a decision to make, but the words of all those in her past who'd made decisions for her battled against her will.

Well, she could make one decision right now, but she wasn't going to make a decision just yet. Before broaching the topic with her clan elders, she had to be certain.

Alistair Sinclair would remain for his recovery for at least a few more days, a week or two if she had her way. But given she knew exactly who he was, the sooner she made a choice, the better. Because she already knew that Alistair was not a man to sit on his laurels. He was a man of action.

THE LAIRD'S GUARDIAN ANGEL

Calliope did not see Alistair again until the evening meal. As he entered the great hall, his gaze seeking out hers, she kept herself steady, eyes on him. Admittedly, she'd been afraid earlier, but now she needed to show him a confidence she wasn't sure she felt. What if he rejected her?

Tucked against her skirts, her hands shook as she nodded to Alistair and then beckoned him to sit beside her at the trestle table. The question in his gaze dissipated, and he marched forward with a swagger and confidence that she recognized.

"I see you're feeling better this evening," she remarked, noticing his freshly shaved face and cleaned-up appearance.

"Amazing what a bath can do," he said with a teasing grin.

"And some fresh air, too. How is your shoulder?"

"Almost good as new."

Calliope smiled. "You are a tough one."

"A good warrior always is." He pulled out her chair with his good arm, and she sat, smiling at his chivalry.

Throughout the meal, they chatted about nothing and everything, getting to know one another better. They teased each other and reminisced about a few funny moments when he'd had a fever.

"Who is Scala?" she asked. "You seemed quite enamored."

Alistair laughed. "Scala was my childhood pup."

"Ah, well, he and you were having quite the game of fetch one night. I almost had to have Duncan restrain you when you grabbed hold of the broth bowl and threatened to throw it to Scala."

Alistair chuckled. "That dog loved to fetch."

"Do you have dogs now?" she asked.

"Aye, several."

Calliope smiled. "My mother hated dogs, so we didn't

have any. But I've always found them to be amazing creatures."

"The next time ye're at Dunbais, I'll introduce ye to my dogs, and if ye want, when we've got a litter, I'll let ye have one."

Warmth and happiness fell over Calliope at that moment. Although she'd never considered getting a puppy of her own, she was already looking forward to the moment she could hold a tiny, soft pup in her arms.

"Cousin, we've found your father."

Calliope glanced up sharply from where she'd been grinding herbs into a paste for Alistair's shoulder. Her hands trembled, and she dropped the pestle against the mortar bowl. She could not have heard that correctly. They'd searched for days. "Where?"

Her cousin Hugh, who she'd played with as a child, looked like he'd seen a ghost. Hugh was nearly the spitting image of her father, his mother being Ramsey's sister. When Calliope's aunt had died in childhood, Hugh had been brought into their home and raised as if he were his son.

"The dungeon," Hugh said.

Calliope closed her eyes and shook her head, devastated all over again. Rather than bury him or even burn his bones, the enemy had simply tossed her father's lifeless body into the dungeon to rot. They'd never checked the dungeon, and he must have been deep within, for when they'd put the English soldiers in the pit for questioning, no one had seen her father then.

But there was no use in putting blame. Why would any of them had thought her father was tossed there in death?

THE LAIRD'S GUARDIAN ANGEL

"He's alive, Calliope. But barely. They found him covered in an old wool sack. 'Tis why we missed him when we did our initial search. We've taken him to his chamber."

"What?" At this bit of news, Calliope's lost her balance, catching herself on the edge of the table. Her vision blurred for a moment, and she blinked to bring herself back. She drew in several steadying breaths, then rushed her cousin, gripping his shirt. "Take me to him."

Hugh nodded gravely, his eyes going to the herbs she'd been grinding behind her. "I think ye're going to want to bring whatever it was ye were making."

"I need to see him first." Then, she could truly assess the situation. From what she'd heard during the moment of attack, he'd been given a death blow, had even claimed the *Sassenach* had killed him. If he'd been left to die for days in the dungeon, it was a miracle he had any breath at all.

Hugh led the way up the castle stairs to her father's bedchamber. Calliope took every step carefully, afraid that at any moment her trembling legs would give out. A wave of fetid air hit them as the bedchamber door was opened. The stench coming from the room was enough to nearly knock her backward. Her hand came to her mouth and nose, tears stung her eyes.

Ramsey lay unconscious on top of the blankets, his clothes bloody, wounds gaping and untended. The sight was enough to make Calliope cry out. Her legs buckled, and she started to fall backward, but someone caught her from behind. Strong arms wrapped around her middle, steadying her, and lifting her back onto her feet. But they didn't let her go, rather held her until she could find her balance once more. She turned around to see Alistair there, gravely staring toward the bed, and she was instantly comforted by his presence.

"I've got ye, lass," he whispered, taking her hand and leading her toward the edge of the bed.

If not for Hugh haven't told her he was alive, she would swear her father was dead. He was the very picture of the aftermath of battle.

"Papa," she whispered, reaching out to touch her father's weathered face.

The man who had done this to him... But she shook away the vengeful thoughts. Now was not the time for her anger but for getting to work. If her father had any chance of survival, it would be up to her.

Calliope straightened her spine, forced herself to find that stoic calm she had when working on the ill. Though she'd never witnessed something this bad, she managed to conjure the strength she would need to take care of her father. He'd been given a second chance at life, and she wasn't about to be the reason he couldn't grasp it.

"I need linens, hot water, whisky, all of my herbs, bandages," her list went on, and people started running to do her bidding. "Knife," she said, holding out her hand.

Alistair placed his own dagger in her hand.

There was no time to lose. Calliope cut away her father's mangled, bloody clothes. There were a few times she had to turn away, fearful of crying or retching, and each time, Alistair put a calming hand on her shoulder, took the knife, and continued the work.

Without him, she wasn't certain how she would have finished.

All through the cleaning of the wounds with hot water and the whisky, her father didn't make a sound. The wounds had all become infected, and there was evidence of rat bites, as well as an infestation of maggots. How could anyone do this to another person... Though she was grateful her father was alive, she was tormented by the thought of what he'd been through.

His chest barely rose and fell, and she held a finger just beneath his nose more than once to see if he was still breathing.

His body was covered in wounds, deep gashes from a blade, and bruises from the fight. Calliope packed the wounds with herbs, sewed them up, and put healing poultices on them, wrapping them tight. Still, he didn't move.

She worked for hours, well into the night, and then she collapsed in a chair beside his bed and fell asleep, only to startle every few minutes to make sure he was still breathing.

This went on for several days. If not for the slow breath coming from her father's nose, she would have thought him dead. By her side always was Alistair until Hugh, Duncan, and Broderick insisted they get some sleep of their own. Each was reluctant to leave. Calliope because she wanted to be there for her father, and Alistair because he wanted to be there for her.

On the third morning, her father stirred, eyes burning with fever. He stared at her as if he'd seen a ghost. "Mary."

"Nay, Papa, 'tis Calliope."

"Calliope..." he whispered before falling unconscious once more.

Nearly a week went by like this, her father hovering on the brink of death. But by day seven, he was awake for several minutes at a time, and they were able to give him broth.

By day eight, he was swatting away Calliope and Bessie's helping hands.

"Papa," Calliope said, taking his hand in hers. She wanted to tell him how scared she'd been. How happy she was that he was alive. But the words caught in her throat.

He patted her hand. "I know, lass, I know. We've both

been through Hell, and now we're getting a second chance at life. No damned *Sassenach* is going to take us down."

Ramsey stared over Calliope's shoulder at Alistair. "Sinclair. Ye have my thanks."

Alistair nodded. "'Tis your daughter who deserves the credit, Ramsey. She escaped to find us, and then she saved us, too."

Ramsey nodded. "I want to hear about that."

Calliope settled into the chair to share the story.

22

During the time they cared for her father, Alistair's health improved significantly. Each day, Calliope thought would be the one he'd say he was headed back to his castle, and yet he'd stayed and helped her with her father, and at the end of each day, they sat beside each other at the trestle table, laughing, sharing stories, and enjoying each other's company.

They'd grown more comfortable with each other over the last few days. And dare she say it, more than comfortable. As Calliope had tended his shoulder wound, he'd had to remove his shirt and sit before her with his bare chest, and she never seemed quite able to find her breath. She tried to focus just on his shoulder, but it was hard to do that when the man was practically bulging with muscle all over.

Really, it seemed pretty unfair to anyone with a pair of eyes that the man should be formed so well, and if she was honest, just thinking about it now brought a blush to her face.

He helped her to understand Scottish customs she'd either forgotten about or knew nothing of and even taught her how to do the Ghillie Callum, a dance over swords that he, Duncan, and Broderick were incredibly skilled at. The entire clan—even her father, who was carried down when he was feeling better to watch—stood around them in a circle until Duncan pulled Bessie into his arms and Broderick, the Cook.

Calliope's happiness grew with each passing day, and so did her sense of belonging. There'd been no more talk of wanting, though there'd been plenty of it. At night, when they went to bed, Alistair would watch her longingly, and she was certain her gaze was mirrored in his. When their fingers brushed, she shivered and wanted more than anything to grab his hand in hers.

Though he didn't try to kiss her anymore, she wouldn't have minded if he did. But he seemed to be waiting for her to make the next move. Completely fair since she'd run away. It also made her feel as though he respected her. Understood that a woman's only bargaining chip was the currency that lay between her legs.

Not that she wanted to think of her body as currency.

And that only made her want to kiss him more. Several times, she'd come close to asking, only to shy away or be interrupted by a clan need or his men who seemed to linger in all the places they went.

But tonight, she was going to ask him to kiss her. She couldn't take the waiting anymore. Knowing that his mouth on hers was all she'd dream about when she went to bed.

Calliope entered the great hall, her head held high, smiling and greeting those of her clan. They no longer asked her about which clan men she wished to wed. They seemed to have given up on that task for now, either because she kept putting them off, or was it because they'd noticed her feelings for Alistair? Or maybe it was because her father was found alive, and they needn't worry about who would be their leader.

She wasn't immune to their stares and whispers, none of which were done with anything other than a smile. And in fact, she found their curiosity encouraging. A sennight ago, she'd told herself she'd have that much time to decide on her future, and Calliope was very close to declaring just what that decision would be. She only hoped her father would give his blessing, for she was still willing to make it if he didn't.

A life with Alistair was what she wanted.

All the decisions that came with what a relationship between them meant she hadn't figured out, but that could come later. What had to come first was how she felt about Alistair. And tonight, after they supped, she was going to share her feelings.

"Wine?" Alistair offered, holding out a cup as they sat down for the evening meal.

"Thank you." My goodness, but her belly was a whirl of nerves.

She took a long sip of the wine he poured, hoping it would bolster her nerves, but it only seemed to make her more nervous.

Alistair served her meal, piling her trencher with meat, fish, bread, and cheese. She picked at each, barely tasting the flavors their Cook had put together, as her mind was on what she planned to do when the meal was over. She was glad her father was not joining them tonight, for if he'd been at the table, she might have lost her nerve.

"Are ye well, lass?" Alistair asked, leaning closer to her.

"Aye. Why?" Oh, why did her voice have to sound so... wobbly?

Alistair gave her an odd look. "Ye've hardly touched your meal."

"Oh," she laughed, shook her head, and stuffed some cheese into her mouth. "My mind is elsewhere tonight."

"Where is it?" he asked, spearing a piece of venison.

"Out there somewhere." She waved toward the door.

"Shall we go and fetch it?" he asked with a conspiratorial grin. "I've heard if ye let the mind run off too far, ye might never get it back."

Calliope laughed. "If I were still in England then I would say let it run. But perhaps you are right, and we should go and seize it before I never get it back." Just like she wanted to seize this moment alone with him.

She pushed back her chair, clearly surprising him as his eyes widened. He dropped his knife, still speared with meat.

"Ye're serious," he said.

"Aye." Calliope lifted her skirts and marched toward the door. It was now or never, and she didn't want to stop her forward progression in case she lost her nerve.

Tonight, she was going to make what she wanted very clear. Calliope was seizing her Fate with her own two hands.

Alistair ignored the teasing calls of his men as he followed Calliope from the great hall.

There'd been a determination in the set of her jaw that had his curiosity blazing. What was the lass up to?

The moment he crossed over the threshold, she grabbed him by the front of his shirt, shut the door, and pushed his back against it. Shocked and even more curious, Alistair held up his hands in surrender and grinned.

"Och, lass, what have I done?"

"Nothing and everything," she said. "Now, do be quiet because I am swiftly losing my nerve."

Her eyes sparkled in the moonlight as her gaze roved over his face, searching for something, and what he wasn't aware. So, he kept smiling, encouraging. He rather liked how she was manhandling him in the moment.

"You have not tried to kiss me in a week."

He nodded because he hadn't thought it was true. "No,' because I have no' wanted to."

"You're not supposed to say anything."

He pressed his lips closed.

"I have wanted you to kiss me. But I wasn't certain it was right. Or that..."

Alistair swallowed. Hard. If she kept talking about kissing, he was liable to take hold of her right now and kiss her until they were both senseless.

"I've never been in charge of my own fate," she said. "But I've decided that I am now. I am not going to allow anyone to make any choices for me—even my father. And I've decided that I do not want to marry a Ramsey."

Alistair nodded slowly, for this was something he'd already figured out when he'd watched the men in her clan attempt to approach her, only for her to sweetly brush them off.

"I am going to marry a Sinclair."

Alistair's entire body stiffened. "Who the hell are ye marrying?" His words came out a growl. Whoever the bastard was, he was going to rip him limb from limb. Calliope was his.

His, goddammit.

Calliope looked startled, eyes widened, her grip on his shirt loosening, and then she was laughing. Doubled over laughing. What the hell was so funny?

"Name him, lass, so I might put him out of his misery."

That only made her laugh harder.

"I swear on all that is holy, he willna live to see the morning."

"Oh, please, I pray, do not go to such an extreme, for then we shall never kiss."

Alistair reared back. "What?"

"'Tis you, you oaf. I want to marry you. I want to kiss you whenever I want for the rest of my life without having anyone tell me I cannot."

Alistair had never been stunned, speechless in his life. He'd chosen to be speechless countless times, but all thought and ability to use his tongue to form syllables had never been an issue for him until this very moment.

"Did you hear me, Sinclair?"

Alistair slowly nodded. "Ye want to marry me."

"Aye."

All the fears he'd had in the past about leaving a wife behind should he die came tunneling back to him at that moment and blurted out on his tongue. "But I could die in battle. Leave ye alone."

Calliope nodded. "I could too. But isn't that more reason to seize this moment? I love you, Alistair Sinclair and I'm not afraid to share that. I'm done hiding behind fear and rules. I want you. I need you."

Something in the center of Alistair's chest burst right then and there. He grabbed Calliope by the waist and tugged her flush to him. "My God, lass, I love ye so much. And I'm going to be afraid of losing ye every day of our damned lives."

"Me too. Now kiss me."

And he did.

23

They were married the next morning, with members of several clans in attendance. When she thought she might get some pushback from her father, he only grinned, nodded, and gave them his wholehearted blessing.

There was much negotiation between the clan elders, but in the end, Calliope made the final choice. She told her father that he should keep Hugh as his heir. After all, he had been the one her father trained for the position, thinking that she'd passed on as a child.

It was only fair that Hugh be given what he'd earned, and she would take her place as Lady Roslin, mistress of Dunbais Castle and Alistair's wife.

The wedding ceremony was short and sweet, and the feast after was incredible. They'd danced over the swords until Calliope thought she might drop. Then she'd given Alistair a look and said, "I think I'd like to kiss you now." Alistair had swept her up in his arms and marched up the stairs of the keep to her bedchamber, where a fire had been lit. Two goblets of wine settled on a table with a platter of biscuits.

"Wine, love?" he asked.

Calliope shook her head. "I want you to kiss me and never stop."

"Never?" Alistair winked.

"Never," she grinned.

"When Lady Roslin issues an order, Baron Roslin must obey."

A teasing glint entered his beautiful eyes. Calliope loved seeing his playful side. Alistair was a man to be reckoned with on the battlefield. He was strong and powerful. Deadly.

And yet, when he touched her and kissed her, he did so with a combination of gentleness and passion that threw her off balance, making her soar. Everything about him made her heart swell with love.

"I order you to kiss me, husband."

"Och, and I hate to disappoint yet." He leaned forward, just a breath away, and whispered, "I'm going to kiss ye until your knees grow weak."

A heated flush swept from the top of her head down to where her knees were already quite weak.

"I await your attentions then," she teased back with a confidence she didn't quite feel, even as she grasped his arms to hold herself upright.

Alistair grinned wickedly. "With pleasure."

Before she could even contemplate a response, he licked her lower lip and tugged it with his teeth. Frissons of hot desire sparked through her core, pooling at her center. Saints, but she was barely standing, and he'd only just begun.

Perhaps, like she had on the front stairs of the castle when she'd asked him to marry her, if she took charge, she'd be more likely to keep her footing. There was no looking back now. Calliope captured Alistair's tongue between her teeth and sucked it into her mouth. Her husband growled a deep vibrating noise that sent a shockwave of pleasure coursing through her.

If this was just a kiss, how was she supposed to survive the wedding night?

Stroking up her arms, Alistair gently massaged her shoulders, her back, the sides of her ribs—and then, with the lightest of touches, the undersides of her breasts.

Her nipples grew taut, and a wicked desire for him to touch them took hold. But

he didn't go near them, and she had no idea if her desire was right or wrong. Her body, however, seemed to know as she thrust her chest forward, seeking more of his sinful caress. But her husband was a tease, and instead of giving in to her silent request, he drove her crazy by stroking everywhere else on her upper body.

Oh, he was good at kissing and touching...very good. They'd barely gotten anywhere, and already she was melting. She was sure her heart was going to stop beating at any moment, so fast was her pulse.

Nay, she thought to herself, I'm in charge.

The only thing was, she had no idea what she was doing. But there was one thing she knew that was necessary between a man and his wife when they made love, and that was that they needed to be naked.

Calliope gently broke their kiss, taking a step away from Alistair, who eyed her with a look of awe and bemusement. His lips were red and wet from their kiss, and it made her whole body clench just to look at him.

She untied the braided belt at her waist without taking her eyes from his. Alistair's gaze followed her movements, and she watched the knob in his neck bob as he swallowed and let out a long, slow breath as if he were doing everything in his power to control himself in this moment.

That subtle move gave her all the confidence she needed to keep going.

With slow, seductive movements, she peeled away every inch of fabric from her body. Watched his eyes widen, then grow heavy. His shoulders and chest rose and fell with his heightened breath. The pulse point in his neck beating hard.

From the look of him, Alistair's desire was growing with each inch of skin she exposed, and a sense of power coursed through her that was even more potent than when she'd sucked his tongue into her mouth.

Calliope tossed her gown aside and stood there in just her chemise, the fabric so thin that her hardened nipples jutted against it. Each dusky nipple was clearly visible, and Alistair's eyes were riveted to the twin spots. She arched her back slightly, letting him see more of her, teasing him as she took hold of the ribbons at the center of her chest.

"Wait," Alistair's voice was husky. "Allow me."

Calliope stilled her fingers, watching, holding her breath as he pinched the ribbons between his thumb and forefinger. With a slow, agonizing pull, he loosened the ribbons, the sound of both their quickened breaths echoing in the room.

The ribbon came unfurled, her chemise falling open to expose her skin to Alistair's view for the first time. Calliope sucked in a breath, her heart pounding as Alistair ran a finger from her throat down to the valley between her breasts, then lower still to circle around the dip of her navel. With every caress of his eyes and finger, her skin sizzled, and she shivered.

"Ye're skin is softer than I could have ever imagined," Alistair whispered.

Sliding a hand around her naked waist, he leaned forward and kissed her collarbone. Calliope gasped at the feel of his lips on her skin, certain she would never know how to breathe properly again after this night.

Alistair trailed his lips, licking her as he went, down between her breasts and pushing the chemise off her shoulders, leaving her top fully exposed to the air and his touch.

"I like the way you touch me," she said.

"Good. I want ye to feel good."

"I do..."

Alistair pulled her taut against him, her naked breasts pressed to the fabric of his shirt. His hands wrapped around her waist, and he brushed his lips over hers. He was gentle at first, making her hotter and hotter. His kiss was sensual, slow, their tongues stroking languidly as though they had all the time in the world to taste one another. And really, they did.

Calliope wanted to feel his skin, too. He wanted to know what it would be like for her breasts to be flush with his chest, with no barrier between them. She gripped the back of his shirt and tugged it free from his plaid, splayed her hands on the bare muscles of his chest, her eyes on the slowly healing wound on his shoulder.

"Does it hurt?" she asked.

"Nay. When I'm kissing ye, I had no' even given it a thought."

Still, she would be careful with him. There were other scars on his chest as she ran her fingers over the hardened ridges of his muscles. Battle wounds. Alistair was a true warrior who had claimed victory hundreds of times.

His skin was warm, hard, pure strength. As she brushed her fingertips over his skin and touched the twin points of his nipples, something ignited inside him. Alistair let out a growl and took her mouth with rousing passion. Oh, but her husband had the power and passion to make her feel weak and strong at the same time.

While she ran her hands up along his spine, Alistair continued his exploration, hands on her belly and back. Anticipation consumed her. She breathed in his alluring scent and pressed her mouth to the skin of his chest. 'Twas as if his scent could leave her undone, and she couldn't get enough. Alistair hissed a breath and tugged her chin up to press his mouth to hers. While he kissed her, she splayed her hands over the rippling expanse of his taut, masculine abdomen. Every part of him was strong. Built to defend, and yet it appeared he was also built to give her pleasure.

"Och, lass..." he murmured, trailing his lips from hers to form a provocative path along her neck.

Her skin lit on fire where his lips touched, and she wanted to extend that blaze to him. Calliope pressed her lips to his corded neck, right where she could feel the pulse of his veins. Another hiss of breath came from Alistair. He licked a trail on the column of her neck, and she mimicked his movements, the tip of her tongue darting against his salty flesh.

Before she could ponder more on how she could torment her husband with pleasure, Alistair cupped her breasts. She held her breath, thrusting her chest forward, silently begging. And he didn't leave her wanting. Alistair brushed his thumbs over her aching nipples.

Calliope gasped a moan. This was what she'd wanted before, needed. And she desired so much more.

Alistair slid his mouth from her neck and kissed between her breasts. She threaded her fingers into his hair as he nuzzled the fleshy mounds. Hot, sensual breath caressed her flesh, and she moaned—a noise she didn't even know she could make. And another desire took hold in her mind. His wicked tongue, which had so expertly licked her neck—she wanted him to do the same to her breasts.

THE LAIRD'S GUARDIAN ANGEL

"Please, Alistair," she begged, uncertain if it was a request that he could even make happen.

But he didn't make her guess or wait.

Searing hot velvet caressed over the tip of her breast. Calliope cried out, eyes flying open to watch with fascination as Alistair's expert tongue flicked over her nipple. Every part of her body swooned and clenched, and she forgot how to breathe. He circled around the tip, flicked his tongue over it, and then blessedly sucked her nipple into his mouth. Calliope moaned, a guttural, feral sound, as her brain abandoned her, leaving her a white, hot, sinful mess.

She held tight where she'd threaded her fingers into his hair and begged him not to stop. To give her more... to give her... she didn't know what, only that she never wanted this pleasure to end.

But then Alistair pulled away and took a step back. "Och, love, I want to be skin-to-skin with ye."

Calliope nodded, wanting very much to feel the same thing. She watched, mesmerized, as Alistair removed his plaid and tossed the long fabric behind him. Alistair, with his golden, muscled skin, was beautiful. The man could have been sculpted from stone; only she knew when she caressed those ridges and lines that his skin was warm. He might look like a marble statue, but he was a hot-blooded man. With his plaid dropped, he was left nude and completely bared to her.

My goodness... Calliope's eyes widened as her gaze narrowed in on that very male part of him that stood at attention, beckoning her.

For the briefest of seconds, she was scared about what would happen. But deep down, she wanted this. Wanted to feel him inside her. Wanted to be loved by him. But how?

"I'm not entirely sure this will work," she said, bemused,

eyeing the center of his body, wanting to reach out and feel him.

"I assure ye, 'twill work perfectly," he said, his voice low, sensual.

Alistair slid his arms around her, pulling her against him. Skin to skin as he'd promised, and she gasped. All hard lines to her much softer ones. Sparks of pleasure and need coursed through her, and once more, she forgot how to breathe.

"Kiss me, wife," he demanded.

While Calliope had thought she wanted to be in charge before, she realized she was more than happy to let her husband take the lead.

While he kissed her, he slid his hand over her back, stroking a burning path from her spine to her buttocks. Calliope shivered and kissed him harder. He massaged her backside, cupping, gripping, tugging her against him so that his hardened shaft pressed to her belly in tantalizing delight. She moaned. He caressed her hip, her bare ribs, belly, the undersides of her breasts, and each touch was soft but so filled her with pleasure and need that she found herself writing against him. Between her thighs grew damp and pulsed with a need she couldn't comprehend.

Before she knew what was happening, Alistair lifted her into the air and laid her on the bed. He slipped his hand between her thighs, gently forcing her to open her legs for him. She did so without hesitation and moaned when he slid a finger through her wet folds and stroked over the hardened nub of her pleasure. Every part of her clenched and trembled. She pushed her hips up, wanting more of the wonderful sensations he was giving.

Then he pushed a finger deep inside her.

Calliope cried out, clinging to him, her body begging for me.

"Do ye like that?" Alistair asked. His voice was deep and alluring, his words sliding over her body with the same pleasure as his fingers.

"Aye." She moaned as he continued to stroke. "But what about you?" she asked, her voice equally husky. "Can't I give you the same pleasure?"

Alistair groaned, his head falling to her forehead.

"Please," she said, "let me."

Alistair guided her hand to grasp the thickness of his shaft, the hardness of his velvet skin filling her palm.

"Oh my," she mused, squeezing.

Alistair hissed. "Gentle, love."

"Like this?" Growing bolder, she stroked up and down, listening to the increased intake of his breath.

※

Alistair gritted his teeth at the warmth of his wife's fingers encircling his cock. No woman had ever made him feel this way. And there'd been no other woman he wanted to please as much. Aye, he was a good and generous lover, but with Calliope, it was different. With her, he wanted to soar to the heavens and back over and over and over and over and over. Maybe never coming down.

Was this the difference between lust and love?

"Ye're going to drive me mad, lass."

"Is that a good thing?" She grinned wickedly up at him as she stroked her thumb over the tip of his erection.

Another few minutes of this, and he was bound to finish right in the palm of her hand. "Och, lass, too good."

"Do you want me to stop?" she asked.

"No' yet." Alistair closed his eyes, giving in to a moment of pleasure. There was something about having her be the one to touch him. This was more than pleasure. More than rutting. This went much deeper. The molding of two hearts. Love, passion. His soul mate.

"Your skin is soft and yet so hard," she said with wonder.

Alistair could only grunt in return because, once again, his wife seemed to have robbed him of the ability to form a coherent thought, let alone words.

"Och, no more," he groaned, "else we'll never get to the good part."

"Do I want the good part?"

Alistair chuckled and caressed her pleasure nub in circles; all the while, her eyes rolled, lips parted. "Aye, lass ye do."

But she didn't stop stroking him either, and he liked it so much he couldn't seem to find the power to make her stop. Somehow, he managed a force of will to remove her hand. "Tease," he said against her earlobe, taking the flesh between his teeth. Alistair nuzzled her neck, loving the hiss of her breath.

"You like that a lot," she said confidently.

"Oh, aye, lass. I liked it verra much."

Calliope sighed, and though he didn't see her face, he sensed her smile. He liked the sounds of her sighs and craved to hear more. He kissed a path between her breasts to her belly, glorying in her beautiful flesh made golden in the firelight.

Her breasts were round, full, perky and just as soft as they looked. Her hips were rounded, thighs long and sculpted, and a triangle of golden hair graced the apex. Alistair stroked over her thighs, running his hands from her knees to her hips.

"Ye're so beautiful," he whispered.

"Thank you."

Alistair parted her thighs, revealing the pink petals of her sex, and his breath caught. When he glanced up at her, Calliope's eyes were heavily lidded, cloudy with desire, and she watched him with the same fire he'd come to recognize as her spirit.

The love he felt for her was enough to overwhelm him. How he never wanted to disappoint her. His chest grew tight, and every muscle coiled, ready to spring. He made a vow to himself right then and there that he would make her cry out with pleasure again and again.

Her features relaxed, and she smiled. "Are ye well, husband?"

"More than well. I am the luckiest man in the world," he answered, winking. "I love ye." He slid his hands up and down her warm thighs.

Calliope sucked her lower lip into her mouth and gripped his arms at the elbows. She tugged. "I love you too."

Alistair knelt between her thighs, feeling the warm length of her shapely legs on his hips. His cock pulsed with need, and if it was even possible, he was harder than he'd ever been before. Calliope's eyes riveted on the place between them where the tip of his shaft pressed to her sex. Her fingers dug into his arms. There was no fear in her gaze, however, only an intense need, desire, and want.

The heat of her body cradling his erection made him wince with unspent pleasure. The potency of his desire for her was enough to make him lose control. Closing his eyes, he laid claim to her mouth, attempting to distract himself from what he really wanted, which was to bury himself deep in her hot center.

Tremors passed through him as she massaged his back, arms, and hips. His control was slipping with every passing second.

Pulling away from her mouth, he kissed his way back toward her lush breasts and then lower. He wanted to taste her, to pleasure her with his mouth. Her feminine scent teased his senses and made his mouth water.

When he kissed the very apex of her thighs, where soft, golden curls began, Calliope gasped and clenched her thighs tight on his head.

"Are you...?"

"Aye."

"Can you...?"

"Oh, aye."

"Oh, my..." She sighed, her thighs falling open in surrender.

He breathed hotly over her folds, listening to her whimper. "I promise ye're going to like it."

"I believe you."

Alistair teased her folds with the tip of his tongue. One glance showed he was indeed enjoying this very much. Alistair dove in for another taste. He teased, probed, licked. Calliope's whimpers grew to full-out cries of pleasure. Oh, how he wanted more. With his thumbs, he pealed her folds open, giving him full access to her nub of pleasure while he made love to her with his mouth. God, she tasted like Heaven. Slick heat and feminine sensuality. He pleasured her nub, flicked his tongue over it, and slid his tongue over her folds.

Calliope's thighs shook, and she clenched tight. Her fist lay buried in his hair, holding his mouth tight to her center. Her hips rose and fell beneath his ministrations. When he slipped a finger inside her hot velvet sheath, her muscles squeezed him tight.

Och, but she was close...

Alistair didn't let up. Continued his ministrations until Calliope's cries of pleasure drew out into cries of release.

"Alistair!" Her body shook and shook beneath him, clenched tight, her fist in his hair giving him a pleasurable pain.

With the strength of her climax, eyes widened, mouth opened in surprise, cheeks flushed pink.

Alistair smiled, a curve of pure male satisfaction. "I told ye, ye'd like it."

Calliope gave a breathless laugh. "Aye... 'Twas... amazing." She licked her lips. "Will you let me do the same to you?"

Alistair's cock pulsed with the thought of her luscious lips wrapped around him. "Next time," he croaked out.

"Oh, do let me have some fun now."

He shook his head. "If I do that, we'll never get to the bedding."

"Oh," she said, nodding. "Then next time."

He slid up her body until they were nose to nose, his length between her thighs, ready to burst.

"I want ye so verra much," he whispered.

Calliope responded by lifting her hips and kissing him. "I'm yours."

That was all the permission he needed to make them one. Alistair tilted his hips, his cock pressing against her slick heat. Slowly, he inched forward, trying to ease into her so he didn't hurt her. And yet he knew, this being her first time, that it was going to hurt no matter what. He only hoped the pain would recede swiftly.

"Kiss me, love," he demanded, taking her mouth with his as he surged forward, burying himself in one swift thrust.

She cried out against his mouth, a different sound than before, this one filled with pain.

"I'm so sorry," he said.

My God, he'd hurt her, and yet Calliope was exquisitely tight, surrounding him at once in a cocoon of heat. Pleasure pulsed through him, and he was in danger of finishing before they even started. His forehead fell against hers, and he couldn't move. He just breathed, trying to focus and push away the release that hovered right on the edge.

"'Tis all right," she said, her voice tight. "We'll soon be to the good part."

Just like her to comfort him in this moment.

"Did it hurt you too?" she asked, shifting beneath him.

"Do no' move, love." He squeezed his eyes shut.

"'Twill be all right," she crooned, shifting again.

"'Tis ye I'm worried about," he said. "I dinna hurt."

"Oh. I feel better now." She lifted her hips. "In fact, that feels quite good," she murmured, moving to kiss his neck.

Relief flooded him. He'd never bedded a virgin before and was glad the pain did not last, for he'd heard nightmares of brides crying all through the ordeal.

And yet his woman... she was taunting him with her mouth. And if she kept doing that... Alistair claimed her mouth if only to stop the heated torture of her lips on his flesh. She tilted her hips, nearly upending him, and he let out such a guttural groan he was confident those on the border could hear it.

Alistair slowly withdrew, then plunged back inside. He tried to keep it languid, wanting to drag out their pleasure. But she felt so damn good... And she was moaning, her fingers clasping around his back, hips rising and falling to meet each thrust. His fiery wife was a natural at making love and encouraged him to let loose everything he thought was important.

He kept his pace and thrusts measured, calculated to draw out her pleasure, but Calliope was writhing beneath him and demanding more, not only with her body but also her words. As soon as he felt her body clench tight and her sex begin fluttering, Alistair knew his intent to make love to her for hours was moot, this woman was his undoing. He gritted his teeth and plunged ahead, riding out her climax.

"Oh, Alistair," she gasped.

Tremors shook her body, and his own shivers took hold, pleasure radiating from the base of his spine and surging forward.

Alistair squeezed his eyes shut as the pleasure took hold of his body and possessed him. Yet, he tried to force it back. Not yet. He pressed his lips to the crook of her shoulder and licked at her skin. Swirling his hips, he arched up inside her, hitting that spot he knew would bring her another release. Calliope gasped and cried out. Their bodies slid with heated passion against one another over and over. He had to hold out just a moment longer.

"Oh!" she cried, her fingers raking down his back. Once more, her body surrounded him in a heated peak.

Alistair did not hold back this time. He quickened his pace, thrusting deep and hard. Like gale force, his climax slammed into him with a power he'd never before known. A heady, low moan escaped his throat as his entire body shook, emptying.

"Calliope!" he roared.

Conscious not to crush her, he held himself on his elbows but left his forehead against her shoulder as he waited for his breathing to steady. Their lovemaking had been everything he wanted and more. Life-altering in its power and potency.

"Calliope," he murmured again, then kissed her lightly on the lips and stroked her flushed cheeks. "That was..."

"Magnificent."

He nodded and kissed her again. Felt his heart soar. "I love ye, lass, more than I know how to express."

"I love you, too."

"My guardian angel," he whispered.

Calliope laughed. "Are you growing soft on me, Sinclair?"

Alistair grinned and kissed her hard. "Nay, love, in fact, I'm growing quite hard."

24

Time no longer existed for Calliope and Alistair. The sun rose, and they ignored it. A soft knock sounded on the door throughout the day, but whenever either of them, wrapped in a sheet, answered, it was only a tray of food for sustenance. They ate, they drank, and they fell back into bed until the sun set again.

They spent the entire day and night in their shared bedchamber and according to Alistair, he would have remained there for another day, week, or year. But after two days, Calliope insisted they come out, else her clan—and her father—no longer looked upon her the same. They'd made love countless times and explored each other so thoroughly Calliope thought Alistair might know her body better than she knew her own.

Upon their entry to the great hall, they were greeted with cheers and whistles from the Ramsey clan, her husband's men, and her father. Calliope's face flamed so hot that she was certain to burst into a fiery blaze that sparked enough to light the nearest hearth.

"Glad ye finally decided to grace us with your presence," her father teased, and Calliope almost ran back up the stairs.

But Alistair only chuckled and winked down at her. "Dinna fash, love, 'tis to be expected."

With her mother having often been so critical, it was going to take a lot for her to get used to not being ashamed and to understand a good tease. Alaric Ramsey rose on shaky legs, using the cane that one of his men had fashioned for him, and approached her and Alistair.

Her father tugged her in for a hug, also something she'd not received often from her mother. "I love ye, lass. I'm so glad that ye're happy. If I could turn time around..."

"Oh, Papa," Calliope said. "Do not fill your mind with regrets and what-ifs. We are here together now, and you are alive. We've both been given another chance at life and with me being just across your lands in Sinclair territory, we will see each other often. There will be plenty of time to catch up and to be grateful for those precious moments we've been gifted."

Her father's eyes softened, watered. "How did ye become so wise?"

Calliope smiled. "I suppose the apple doesn't fall far from the tree."

"Am I the tree?" he asked.

She laughed. "Aye, and no one can cut you down."

"Certainly no' an Englishman."

Calliope hugged her father once more, faint memories of him having done so when she was a child filtering warmly back into her mind.

They ate their supper in jovial camaraderie. The stark contrast between how her life had been for years and now was enough to make Calliope pause and reflect. She'd never known what she was missing. And now she couldn't imagine not having a meal without rowdy conversation and laughter. How had she survived so many years in formal, disciplined silence?

"Cousin," Hugh said from down the long trestle table. "I dinna know if ye recall, but it is I who taught ye to climb. Fancy a challenge?"

Calliope laughed, setting down her eating knife and leaning forward on her elbows on the table. "What sort of challenge? For you see, cousin, I have moved on from trees to scaling walls."

"Nay," Alistair boomed. "Nay, nay, nay. Ye canna climb any more walls."

"Do you forbid it?" she contested.

Alistair chuckled. "Forbid ye from doing something? Nay, I would never. Ye'd only make it your purpose to do it all day."

"This is true."

"I merely beg mercy, for if I were to watch ye scale another wall, I'd die of heart failure."

"Then perhaps you should remain at the bottom to catch me."

Alistair groaned. "Fine. But can ye at least grant me the mercy of making it a short wall?"

Calliope grinned mischievously. "What is short to some is tall to others."

Alistair pressed his forehead into his hands with mock exaggeration.

"Wait," Hugh said. "I'm no' certain I'm prepared to scale a wall."

"Without a rope," Calliope added.

"Aye, no' at all." Hugh shook his head.

"I'll teach you," she promised with a nod.

"Perhaps we shall wait on our wager."

"Why no' a tree then?" Ramsey suggested. "Hugh, if ye're to be my heir, ye canna retreat from a challenge."

The conversation continued until it was decided that they'd climb trees on the morrow, and whoever reached the top first won. The prize was any horse from Ramsey's stable, and Calliope knew just the one she wanted.

After supper, there was more dancing, storytelling, and a few games of bones. Alistair kept hinting they should leave, and while her body begged her to let him whisk her up the stairs and fill the rest of her night with pleasure, Calliope insisted they wait until nearly the last of the Ramseys and Sinclairs had gone to bed before retiring, fearful everyone would find her to be entirely too eager to bed her husband.

Which she was. Every glance, every touch—including his hand on her thigh while she supped—was enough to drive her mad.

Calliope beat Hugh three times out of three on the tree climb the following morning and claimed her horse. A dappled mare she named Serena II.

Nearly a sennight of marital bliss passed before Alistair asked if she was ready to return to his castle so his own clan might celebrate their marriage. His patience had been much appreciated by her since she'd been enjoying getting to know her father again. Alistair was so incredibly thoughtful and did not have a selfish bone in his body. Calliope had her trunks packed and handed over the reins to her cousin Hugh within an hour.

The hardest part was leaving her father. He was healing well, a robust warrior who didn't seem to notice his own age. She hugged him tight, with promises from them both to visit often.

THE LAIRD'S GUARDIAN ANGEL

She hugged Gregor and Bessie goodbye and thanked them all for welcoming her with open arms.

Serena II was saddled, but Calliope chose to ride with her husband, not yet ready to be apart. The ride to Dunbais was quite different than the last time Calliope had ridden with Alistair. For one, she was no longer afraid. Blissfully married, in the arms of her husband. Every time she shifted on the horse, this time around, he told her exactly what she was doing to him. Whispering naughty things in her ear that made her want to shove him into the woods and out of earshot of his men while she ravished him—which she did exactly thrice.

When they finally arrived at Dunbais, both were flushed and disheveled, and his men couldn't wait to get away from them.

As she'd come to know him, the clan elder, Augie, greeted them with a wide smile. "I never thought we'd see this lad wed."

"I'm your laird, no' a lad," Alistair said, and though his voice was stern, there was a little curve to his lip that belied his irritation.

"All the same, it appears ye've been conquered by a lass. Our fierce and mighty Sinclair."

"I'd say we conquered each other," Calliope said with a wink in Alistair's direction. And she planned to conquer him again in about five minutes.

CALLIOPE AND ALISTAIR WERE SEQUESTERED IN THEIR chamber less than an hour later. Alistair had ordered them a steaming bath and a meal, which had been delivered swiftly: a table full of sliced apples, bread, cheese, and roasted chicken.

"Are ye hungry, lass?" Alistair asked.

Calliope grinned. "Not for food."

"And the bath?" he asked. There was a mischievous glint in his eyes, and all she could do was imagine what it would be like to sink beneath the surface, their bodies sliding over one another.

"Aye, that sounds divine."

Steam rose from the bath, which one of the maids had sprinkled with dried lavender.

They stripped each other down, and once Alistair was in the shallow tub, water, barely covering his knees, he held out his hand to her. She stepped gingerly into the scented warmth, sinking down onto his lap. The tub was overlarge, one that Alistair had ordered made after spending too many years cramped in a wooden barrel to wash. And yet, the water had not been filled, and she rather liked that for what she had in mind.

"Are ye happy, lass?" Alistair asked.

"Beyond happy," she whispered, leaning her head against his shoulder.

Alistair tipped her chin for a sensual kiss. They gently washed each other between kisses, and she was sure to be careful of Alistair's shoulder, which had healed into a pink scar.

"Promise me every day will be like this," she asked.

"I can promise ye that every day we're together 'twill be like this."

She nodded, knowing there would be times when they were apart. There was no use in pretending that Alistair was not the border guardian, and they lived in hostile times. But she was more than happy to accept that the moments of bliss they would have together would be full of joy.

"When do you have to leave?" she asked.

"No' for some time, lass. I promise."

As a gift, her father had made a deal with Alistair that he would take the next several rounds of border protection at the castle on the River Tweed, which meant they had nearly two months before then. And really, that wasn't something she wanted to think about now. She'd much rather enjoy the pleasure this bath was affording her—and the pleasure she knew her husband could give her.

Calliope's thighs quivered as she turned in Alistair's arms to straddle his hips, the hardness of his shaft pressing enticingly to the bundle of firing nerves in her core. With a boldness she'd grown to embrace, she gripped his length, stroking his hardness, relishing his moans of pleasure and the way his hips jerked in rhythm with her hand.

The desire to taste him was nearly overwhelming. To give him the same rapture his mouth had given her. Calliope shifted back to kneel between his knees.

"What are ye doing, lass?" Alistair's eyes heavily lidded, watching her.

Calliope grinned, feeling like a seductress. "I want to taste you. Remember when you said next time... But you never did let me."

Alistair's eyes widened then, and he sat up a little taller. "Aye..."

"I'm not taking no for an answer this time, husband."

"I willna stop ye." His voice was gruff and so full of sensuality that Calliope shivered.

Calliope stared down at his shaft, thick and hard, and licked her lips. She glanced up at her husband with a sultry gaze as she lowered her head, pressing her lips to the tip of his masculinity.

Alistair groaned and threaded his fingers gently through her hair, a gentle massage that silently begged for more. The skin of his arousal was hot, soft against her mouth.

Calliope flicked her tongue out over the tip, swirling around and around, recalling vividly all the various moves he'd used on hers. She licked him up and down, all the while stroking with her fingers. As his moans and gentle pushes grew more insistent, she opened her mouth and took him inside, all the way to the base.

The primal moan that came from Alistair's mouth was enough to make Calliope's entire body shudder. Between her thighs pulsed, and embers of pleasure lit throughout her limbs. She'd not expected that making love to Alistair with her mouth would fill her with so much desire, need, want.

"Och, wife," he growled. "That feels so good. I need ye to stop. Please..."

"Mmm..." she moaned around his turgid flesh, grinning with an intoxicating power. Not on his life.

"Lass," the word was a hiss and his grip on her hair pushed and pulled as if he couldn't make up his mind. "Please, I want..."

He moaned again and, this time, succeeded in pulling himself out of her mouth.

Alistair lifted her from the tub and carried her over his shoulder toward the bed with a playful smack on her bare behind, then tossed her onto the coverlet.

Calliope erupted in laughter as she fell to the soft mattress, but the moment Alistair spread her thighs and crawled up her body like a man on a sensual mission, her laughter turned to a whimper of pleasure.

"I love you," she whispered as his mouth settled on hers.

Alistair was all strength, hardness, and pleasure as he

pressed his body to hers. "I love ye too," he declared as he thrust home.

Calliope was never going to grow tired of hearing those words. Never tired of her husband desiring her. Never tired of him wanting to give her every ounce of pleasure he could until her entire body was wrung out. The love she had in her heart swelled her entire chest to the point where she sometimes felt she couldn't breathe, that she might just burst from happiness.

With her arms around his neck, she pulled his mouth to hers and gave him all the love she had with her kiss. Their lovemaking was a slow, deliberate pleasure. Alistair kissed her mouth and then her neck, breasts, fingertips. There was not an inch of her left untouched, not a part of her that did not sing for more of his kiss, more of this pleasure.

To think, to know that every night and every day was going to be filled with Alistair, gave Calliope such hope for her future. Before now, she'd been certain that she was going to be chattel, sold to Bryce, or the next highest bidder. A woman who would host dinners, attend court, and produce heirs. Nothing of her own, not even to herself.

But now, all of that had changed. She'd escaped that life to find Alistair, and in turn, he had given up a life of loneliness, betting on her and happiness together.

As their bodies soared to new heights of pleasure and they whispered words of love, the world around them faded. Their love was all-consuming, as if they had risen to another plane just by being together.

When the pleasure grew to be too intense, and the need for release had them both frenzied for satisfaction, Alistair increased his pace. She met him thrust for thrust, tilting her hips until they were both crying out in rapture.

Sated, sweaty, and smiling, they curled into each other's embraces, waiting to return to earth.

Calliope traced a heart on Alistair's chest, smiling as she did so. "I think I am the happiest woman in the world."

"And I am the happiest man. Especially since ye promised no' to climb any more walls." He grinned teasingly.

Calliope issued a mocking gasp. "I promised no such thing."

EPILOGUE

"My lord, there's a messenger here, says he's from the king."

Sir Edgar of Bromley sat up straighter in his chair before the hearth, his near-empty cup of wine quickly refilled by the servant who'd interrupted his drunken mid-day nap. She was a saucy wench, always pretending she didn't like it when he pinched her bottom, just like now. He chuckled and promised to give it to her harder later, to which she played hard to get with a frown.

Edgar had yet to be paid by King Edward for his service of dispatching his sham of a wife, Lady Mary, and delivering his pretend stepdaughter back to Scotland. By now, she must be married to the English lord who'd been sent there to fetch her. The English king had after all insisted that Ramsey, her true father, be the one to agree to the marriage so there could be no skirmish over it. All a waste of time really.

But, at last, he was to be paid! He could practically feel the cold coins in his palms as he imagined sifting through the bottomless, heavy coffer.

Edgar jumped from his chair, spilling his now full cup of wine, but ignoring the mess. He was a landed knight, and landed men didn't clean up their own messes.

The servant who'd awakened him knelt to mop up the wine. He reached forward just for one touch of her rear but remembered the reason she'd woken him in the first place. Instead of a good bottom squeeze, Edgar rushed toward the front entrance of his castle to greet the messenger and, no doubt, take a fat load of coins off his hands.

But when he arrived, the messenger standing before him was nearly twice as tall and four times as wide as any envoy he'd ever come across. There was a fearsome look about him, as though he'd spent hours training for battle, or else he'd spent many a day robbing people on the road. Soldier or outlaw, there was no doubt in Edgar's mind that this was not a messenger. Edgar tried to suppress his shudder, glad he wasn't holding his wine cup, which would no doubt be sloshing all over the sides.

"Who are you?" Edgar demanded. He'd discovered early on in life that if he pretended not to be afraid and instead put out, he would often feel the same way. A necessary tactic at this moment when he was indeed quite frightened by this alarming stranger.

Cold eyes stared down at him, and Edgar puffed his chest to show he wasn't scared, even though he was terrified and close to emptying his bladder right into his hose.

"Ye dinna recognize me?"

Edgar blustered at the offensive Scottish brogue. "A savage in my house? How did you cross the border without being seen?" This was preposterous. How in the hell had a Scot gotten through all the way to his holding, and how did he even know where he was?

THE LAIRD'S GUARDIAN ANGEL

Now, his anger was well and truly overshadowing his fear. This was indeed so outrageous that he might—

The massive Scot laughed, interrupting the internal monologue rushing through Edgar's head.

"Och, but ye think name-calling will have me turning on my heel, Sir Edgar? I'll ask again if ye recognize me."

The more he spoke, the more recognizable he became, and Edgar vividly remembered coming across him on the road in Scotland. "Nay, I do not know who you are," Edgar lied. And I don't care," he lied again. You'll need to leave. I've no business with the Scots."

How could his maid have gotten this so clearly wrong? This was no emissary, and he wasn't even English. He'd have to punish her for this mistake. Idiots had no place in his household. Though he would greatly miss her bottom.

"Och, but ye do, man," the Scot said. "We've much business. Let's start with the abduction of Lady Mary and her daughter."

"I did no such thing; she came willingly." He crossed his arms protectively over his chest.

"Let's continue with Lady Mary's murder."

Edgar went pale then; he couldn't help it. Part of the reason he was already drunk and not even past noon was because he was certain Mary was haunting him for what he'd done to her. She came to him at all hours of the day, whether he was awake or dead. Accusing him of her murder. Accusing him of treachery. All true, but still.

"Ah, I see we're getting somewhere."

"None of your business," was all Edgar could think to say.

"No' exactly," the Scot replied. "Shall we finish with how ye sent Lady Calliope to witness her father's death? How she was to be next?"

Now Edgar shook his head hard, so hard his cheeks flapped embarrassingly. "Nay, nay, that is not true at all."

The Scot cocked his head. "Ye seem to believe that lie."

"Because 'tis true. Lord Ellington was to go there for payment and marry her."

"Lord Ellington, ye say?"

"Aye. He was to go there for payment and to collect her. The king's orders."

The Scot grunted. "If what ye say is true, then he disobeyed his king's orders and paid the ultimate price for it."

If it were possible to lose more blood from the head than he already had, Edgar drained right then and there. He backed up a step if only to gain his balance against the wall. The cold stone did little to comfort him. However, he did not fall.

"And why have you come?" he asked, already knowing the answer.

The Scot grinned. "There is a price to pay for what ye've done, too."

"You cannot kill me!" Edgar shouted.

The Scot looked at him oddly. "I could."

"You cannot! My servants will hear."

"Likely they will, but I've already given them quite a bit of coin to start off on their own. Ye see I consider this a wedding gift to my wife."

"Your wife?" Edgar shook his head. None of this was making any sense whatsoever.

"Aye. Lady Calliope is my wife, and she has asked me to bring ye to her to face your Fate."

Edgar dropped to his knees. He hadn't even noticed the moment his legs buckled, but he felt the sharp pain of the stones as they cut into his knees upon falling. "She wants to kill me?"

THE LAIRD'S GUARDIAN ANGEL

The Scot shrugged. "I suggested the plow. But she said ye've never worked a day in your life."

Edgar was not going to work a plow; he'd rather die. Knowing he was about to be taken for a serf, he stood quickly, managed to find renewed strength, and turned and ran. Up the stairs to the castle. He barricaded himself in his room, pacing back and forth. He could wait out the Scot. Wait for reinforcements. Certainly, not all of his servants could be paid off with coin.

A soft knock sounded on the door, softer than any Scot.

"Go away!" he shouted.

"But, sir, your wine."

"Oh, my wine." He was quite thirsty. All this running and pacing and worrying. The Scot had given him a real fright.

Edgar marched to the door, yanked it open, and found his cup of wine on the floor beside a flagon for a refill. Thank goodness, no Scot was in sight.

Relieved not to have to face the giant just yet, he picked up the cup, drained it, and then refilled it.

He was dead before he took another sip.

※

By the time Alistair returned from his impromptu trip to England, his brothers and their wives, his sisters Iliana and Matilda, and her husband were all at Dunbais. They rushed from the keep to greet him in the courtyard, all smiles and teasing, the way he loved it.

He'd only been gone a few weeks, but it was long enough for him to greatly miss being at home—and most of all, he missed his wife fiercely. Calliope barreled into him, and he lifted her in the air for a twirl as he pressed his lips to hers. They took a great bit of teasing for such a public display, but

Alistair didn't care. He loved his wife and wasn't scared to show it.

"Where is Edgar?" Calliope asked, looking to the men behind him and not seeing her wicked stepsire.

"Well, I did try to apprehend him," Alistair frowned, recalling the coward who'd dropped to his knees. He'd never understand what Lady Mary had seen in the man. "But it appears he made his own enemies. He was poisoned by a servant."

"Poisoned?" Calliope looked stunned.

"Aye."

Calliope narrowed her eyes. "And you had nothing to do with it?"

Alistair chuckled. "Unfortunately, nay. I wanted to tear him limb from limb, the coward. But he hid from me and then succumbed to a single poisoned cup of wine." Alistair shrugged.

Calliope shook her head; her look of surprise changed to one of understanding. "Well, he wasn't always nice to the servants. I suppose I shouldn't be surprised. And I suppose that's better than him trying to work a plow. We'd likely lose an entire harvest."

"They were very easily swayed to tell him I was an envoy from the English king. To be honest, I was quite surprised it all worked so easily and swiftly. And he is now in Hell being punished for his sins. Your mother's death, what he did to ye, 'tis avenged."

"Where he belongs. My poor mother. She was not always the easiest to get along with, but I loved her, and she did not deserve to be killed by him." Calliope nodded grimly, and then her demeanor changed. "Your family! They are such a delight."

"I've missed them greatly."

THE LAIRD'S GUARDIAN ANGEL

Not a moment too soon, Alistair was surrounded by all those in his life he loved. He was getting ribbed by his brothers for marrying, getting coddled by his brother's wives, who adored him, getting a jab to the ribs from Iliana, who said she wanted to be at the wedding, and getting a big hug from Matilda, who wished him every happiness.

Alistair stared down at his beautiful wife, a gift he'd never thought he'd have. A woman to love and be loved by in return. His guardian angel saved him from a lonely Fate. Never once had Alistair thought this was what he would want until he almost didn't have it.

With his arm outstretched, he pulled Calliope to him, and she fell against him with a radiant smile. "I love ye, wife. Ye've made my life complete."

Calliope pressed her hand over his heart. "I love you, too." She leaned up, brushing her lips over his. "Now, let us feast and dance. Douglass and Rhiannon have challenged me."

"Challenged?"

"Aye, they think they can dance swords better than me. I aim to show them they are wrong."

Alistair's head fell back as he laughed.

"And another thing," Calliope said, giving him a poke in the chest. "You didn't tell me about Douglass and Rhiannon."

"I most certainly did."

She shook her head. "Not that your brothers had English wives, aye, you did mention that. But you never gave me their names. I recognized them the moment we met."

"Ye know each other?"

"Aye!" Calliope squealed. "We met every year at the border festival. We became great friends. Is that not the most glorious thing you've heard?"

Alistair grinned and kissed her on top of her head. "Aye, love, the most glorious."

Calliope's happiness was always paramount to him; he hoped she would get along with his brothers' wives. Knowing they were friends before now was a boon Alistair had never counted on.

Could life get any better than this?

ABOUT THE AUTHOR

Eliza Knight is an award-winning and USA Today bestselling author.

Her love of history began as a young girl when she traipsed the halls of Versailles and ran through the fields in Southern France. She can still remember standing before the great golden palace, and imagining what life must have been like. Join Eliza (sometimes as E.) on riveting historical journeys that cross landscapes around the world.

While not reading, writing or researching for her latest book, she chases after her three children. In her spare time (if there is such a thing...) she likes daydreaming, wine-tasting, traveling, hiking, staring at the stars, watching movies, shopping and visiting with family and friends.

She is the creator of the popular historical blog, History Undressed and a co-host on the History, Books and Wine podcast.

She lives on the Suncoast with her own knight in shining armor, three princesses, two very naughty Newfies, and a turtle named Fish.

Visit Eliza at http://www.elizaknight.com or her historical blog History Undressed: www.historyundressed.com. Sign up for her newsletter to get news about books, events, contests and sneak peaks: https://elizaknight.com/news/!

- facebook.com/elizaknightfiction
- x.com/elizaknight
- instagram.com/elizaknightfiction
- bookbub.com/authors/eliza-knight
- goodreads.com/elizaknight

Printed in Great Britain
by Amazon